I0732672

Books by Tina Folsom

Samson's Lovely Mortal (Scanguards Vampires, Book 1)

Amaury's Hellion (Scanguards Vampires, Book 2)

Gabriel's Mate (Scanguards Vampires, Book 3)

Yvette's Haven (Scanguards Vampires, Book 4)

Zane's Redemption (Scanguards Vampires, Book 5)

Quinn's Undying Rose (Scanguards Vampires, Book 6)

Oliver's Hunger (Scanguards Vampires, Book 7)

Thomas's Choice (Scanguards Vampires, Book 8)

Silent Bite (Scanguards Vampires, Book 8 1/2)

Cain's Identity (Scanguards Vampires, Book 9)

Luther's Return (Scanguards Vampires, Book 10)

Blake's Pursuit (Scanguards Vampires, Book 11)

Fateful Reunion (Scanguards Vampires, Book 11 1/2)

John's Yearning (Scanguards Vampires, Book 12)

Ryder's Storm (Scanguards Vampires, Book 13)

Damian's Conquest (Scanguards Vampires, Book 14)

Grayson's Challenge (Scanguards Vampires, Book 15)

Lover Uncloaked (Stealth Guardians, Book 1)

Master Unchained (Stealth Guardians, Book 2)

Warrior Unraveled (Stealth Guardians, Book 3)

Guardian Undone (Stealth Guardians, Book 4)

Immortal Unveiled (Stealth Guardians, Book 5)

Protector Unmatched (Stealth Guardians, Book 6)

Demon Unleashed (Stealth Guardians, Book 7)

Ace on the Run (Code Name Stargate, Book 1)

Fox in plain Sight (Code Name Stargate, Book 2)

Yankee in the Wind (Code Name Stargate, Book 3)

Tiger on the Prowl (Code Name Stargate, Book 4)

A Touch of Greek (Out of Olympus, Book 1)

A Scent of Greek (Out of Olympus, Book 2)

A Taste of Greek (Out of Olympus, Book 3)

A Hush of Greek (Out of Olympus, Book 4)

Venice Vampyr (Novellas 1 – 4)

Teasing (The Hamptons Bachelor Club, Book 1)

Enticing (The Hamptons Bachelor Club, Book 2)

Beguiling (The Hamptons Bachelor Club, Book 3)

Scorching (The Hamptons Bachelor Club, Book 4)

Alluring (The Hamptons Bachelor Club, Book 5)

Sizzling (The Hamptons Bachelor Club, Book 6)

Tiger - on the Prowl

Code Name Stargate #4

Tina Folsom

1

Olivia Morikawa shut down her laptop and closed the lid, before getting up from her desk in her small two-bedroom cottage in Alexandria, Virginia. She used the second bedroom as an office, and had furnished it accordingly, complete with a hidden safe in the back of the closet. She placed her laptop as well as the external hard drive in the safe now, then locked it, and slid the cedar paneling over it, so nobody would even know it existed. She hung the bridesmaid's dress for her sister's upcoming wedding in front of it, before closing the door.

Olivia was normally not a paranoid person, but ever since her sci-fi novels had taken off and were rivaling the great writers of the genre, unseating them from the top spots on the bestseller lists, she'd started worrying about somebody finding out who was behind the male pseudonym T.R. Harland. Her fans were anxious about the next book, and speculations were rife about which main character would get axed next by way of a spectacular death. Her publisher had informed her that two rival authors were actively trying to find out how the *Galaxy Outcast* series was going to continue, and would pay good money to leak spoilers in an attempt to turn her fans against her before the book was even published.

Luckily, so far, nobody had figured out that T.R. Harland wasn't a bearded geek who preferred the company of the people in his head to real-life people, but a somewhat shy 28-year-old woman of Hawaiian descent with a master's degree in fine arts and a fondness for croissants and animals of all kinds. She hoped her secret would never be revealed.

Even her publisher didn't know who she was. She dealt with them only via email and text messages, and any payments she received went to the LLC she'd set up to hide her true identity. At first, she'd done it, because the sci-fi genre was dominated by male authors, and without a track record, she'd figured that no publisher would even take a look at her manuscript if they knew she was a woman. Besides, readers and other authors not knowing who T.R. Harland really was added a certain mystique. Olivia wasn't looking for public adoration. All she wanted was to get lost in her stories and share them with the world.

The only people who really knew what she did, were her parents and her sister, Grace. In fact, she often brainstormed with Grace, and talked to her about her writing when she got stuck, running different scenarios by her to get feedback.

The doorbell pulled her out of her thoughts.

"Olivia?"

"Coming, coming!" she called out toward the door, snatched her workout bag and her yoga mat, and hurried to the door. She opened it.

"Hey, Claire," she said to the woman who was only two years younger than her. "I'm not late, am I?" She waved her to step inside.

Like Olivia, Claire was dressed in yoga pants and a tight top, a small bag slung across her torso, a yoga mat under her arm. Her long red hair was bound back in a ponytail. "No, no, we've still got a few minutes."

"I just need my keys," Olivia said and looked around the foyer, when she spotted them on the shoe bench. "And my phone." She ran back into the office and found her cell phone on the desk.

When she returned to the hallway, she found Claire looking in the mirror, adjusting her hair.

"You look great as always," Olivia said.

Claire chuckled. "It's hard work."

"As if." Olivia shook her head.

"Is that a new outfit?" Claire asked.

"Oh this old thing?" Olivia replied, pointing to the brand-new yoga pants and the pink top she'd bought only days earlier.

Claire rolled her eyes. "Looks good on you. I'm sure Jay will like it."

Olivia felt herself blush.

"Oh, come on, do you really think that no one noticed that you have a huge crush on the guy? Everybody in class knows."

Olivia sighed. "Yeah, everybody but Jay."

Claire shrugged. "Men can be so dense sometimes. Particularly the yummy ones."

"He is yummy, isn't he?" Olivia said.

Looking at the clock in the foyer, Olivia motioned to the door, and she and Claire left the house and started walking.

The moment Olivia had seen Jay enter the yoga room at the *Namaste Studio and Gym* three months earlier, her heart had started beating out of control. At first, she couldn't even believe that Jay was the new yoga teacher. He didn't look like the kale-eating, vegan, thin yoga instructors the studio normally employed. Jay was a tall, muscular guy, who looked more like a kickboxer or a weightlifter than a man who taught yoga to a bunch of housewives, stressed-out professionals, and retirees who tried to remain limber. In his yoga pants, Jay looked like a ballet dancer with strong thighs and slim hips. But his upper body was much bigger than a dancer's, with a broad muscled chest, and strong arms. His skin was a deep brown, and during class she'd often seen a thin sheen of perspiration on it and wanted nothing more than to lick it off him.

"I figure, why not. Olivia?"

Claire's voice pulled her out of her reverie. She hadn't heard a word of whatever Claire had been talking about. "What?"

"I said you have to do something about it. Clearly, he's not gonna ask you out because you're his student. So you have to make the first move. And if you don't ask him out today, I'm gonna do it for you."

They stopped in front of the studio, and Olivia looked at her friend. "What if he says no?"

"Then at least you know. But there's no reason why he wouldn't wanna go out with you. You're pretty, you're smart. What's not to like? Hell, I'd go out with you if I were a lesbian."

"Very funny!"

"Honestly, just put on your big girl pants and ask him," Claire urged her and opened the door to *Namaste*.

Inside the gym, they both signed in, then walked to the yoga room. Outside the door, they took off their shoes, and left their bags in one of the open lockers.

When they entered with their yoga mats, several other students were already assembled, their yoga mats laid out in an orderly pattern. Unfortunately, the first row was already taken, so Olivia had to place her mat in the second row. Clearly, she wasn't the only one who lusted after Jay. The middle-aged housewives in the first row weren't immune to his charm either. When the door opened again behind her, the four women in the first row turned their heads.

Were they wearing make-up? For a yoga class? How pathetic. Olivia sighed, but didn't turn her head to see who'd entered, trying not to make it too obvious that she couldn't wait for Jay to arrive.

From her seated position, gaze downward, she caught a glimpse of the instructor's bare feet as he walked to the front of the class. They were white. She lifted her head and stared at him. This wasn't Jay.

"Morning, all. I'm Mathias. I'll be filling in for Jay today." The pale, spindly guy who couldn't be older than twenty-five set his drink bottle next to his yoga mat. Yep, that was definitely a kale shake.

Disappointment swept through Olivia.

"That's the second week now," Claire whispered next to her.

Olivia glanced at her. "Do you think he's sick?"

Claire shrugged.

"Let's start with some deep breathing this morning," Mathias said.

The entire hour Olivia went through the motions, not really enjoying the exercises like she did when Jay taught the class. Instead of feeling relaxed and invigorated, she felt worried and stressed. She couldn't wait for the class to end, and the moment Mathias released the class with the customary *Namaste*, she was already at the door. Rapidly, she put on her sneakers, grabbed her possessions, and went to the front desk.

Amber, the owner of the studio stood behind the computer.

"Hey, Olivia, good session?" she asked.

"Yeah thanks, though, I'm surprised Jay wasn't teaching. Nothing against Mathias," she added, not wanting to let Amber think that the replacement instructor wasn't any good. "But I just like the way Jay teaches the class. Is he sick?"

Amber let out an annoyed huff. "Your guess is as good as mine. He hasn't been answering his phone. Frankly, I'm so pissed at him that if he does finally call me back, he can look for another studio. I need reliable people."

"Oh," Olivia said. "Maybe something happened to him?"

Amber shrugged. Then the phone rang, and she picked it up.

Now more worried than disappointed, Olivia went outside. A moment later, Claire caught up with her.

"So what's wrong with Jay?" Claire asked.

"Amber didn't know. Apparently, he's not

answering his phone. I have a bad feeling about it. What if something happened to him?"

"You mean like an accident?" She shook her head. "If that were the case, I'm sure somebody would have notified the studio." Then she grimaced. "People are flakes. Better you find out now. Or do you really want a guy who's gonna ghost you after he got what he wanted?"

"Of course not, but he never struck me as a flake."

No, Jay was the serious kind of guy. Almost a little buttoned-up, and she couldn't imagine that he would not show up for his class without an explanation. Not for two weeks in a row. Something was wrong. But how could she figure out what?

2

The huge contraption—which looked like an MRI machine but was something much more dangerous—made a noise like an airplane engine with Jay right in front of it, unable to escape. They'd drugged him and tied him to the gurney, his head in a helmet. He couldn't move a muscle, not even his pinkie. His entire body was paralyzed, while he drifted in and out of consciousness. Around him, several men in lab coats were busy adjusting this or that, conversing with each other. Medical jargon drifted to him, but he didn't need to understand the words. He knew what would happen.

He tried to fight it. But he had no strength.

The face of his tormentor hovered over him, goading him, laughing in that insidious way only cartoon villains did. The laugh was like an echo that bounced off the walls of the enormous hall he found himself in. Jay smelled the dust and the musty scent of something rotting. He smelled wood too, and the strong whiff of an expensive cologne. Smith's cologne.

The gurney Jay was shackled to moved underneath him, and the sound of the machine became even louder, as his head approached the center of the machine. He could only imagine what it would do to him. But he knew he wouldn't survive it. He felt it the instant the huge circular machine started spinning around his head. It felt like a magnet was trying to suck every last cell from his brain.

He wanted to scream, but he couldn't. His vocal cords were paralyzed too. But inside his head, he was screaming, screaming for them to let him out, screaming for somebody to free him. But the pain only magnified, until he could take it no longer, and everything exploded.

Jay shot up to sit and realized that he was in a bed. He was bathed in sweat, and it took him a few seconds to remember where he was. Safe. Rescued by his fellow Stargate agents. They'd freed him in the eleventh hour. A moment longer in the machine, and he would have ended up like Thomas, a Stargate agent Smith had captured before Jay: his brain fried, his other organs unable to function any longer. With a trembling hand, Jay stroked over his head. The indentations from the probes they'd attached after shaving his already short hair, were gone now, but the nightmares remained. He hadn't mentioned them to Ace, Fox, or Yankee, his three rescuers. They couldn't help him with that part of his recovery, though they'd helped him with everything else.

Ace and his fiancée, Phoebe, had offered him a room in their large mansion on the outskirts of Washington D.C. It had once belonged to Henry Sheppard, the CIA agent, who'd created and overseen the top-secret

Stargate program. His own cover as a yoga instructor in a small gym in Alexandria with all likelihood blown, Jay had nowhere else to go, and had accepted the generous offer. Yankee and his girlfriend, Lilly, also lived under Ace's roof; only Fox and his girlfriend, Michelle, lived in a safe house in D.C., but spent most of their days in the mansion working on setting up surveillance operations and anything else that would help the ex-agents find the people responsible for the destruction of the Stargate program and the murder of their leader.

Jay got out of bed and showered. He felt better after it. But he still hadn't found his inner peace. The nightmare of what he'd been through had been disturbing his sleep every night since his rescue ten days earlier. He grabbed the yoga mat Michelle had ordered for him and made his way downstairs. He heard voices and the sound of dishes clanging in the kitchen, but turned toward the back of the house instead. He opened the French doors to the terrace and stepped outside. The air was still fresh, but in a few hours, heat and humidity would engulf all of Washington D.C.

Jay spread out his yoga mat on the terrace and stood in mountain pose, his eyes closed, as he collected his thoughts. In the last three years, ever since he'd had to go on the run after Henry Sheppard's murder so he wouldn't become the next victim, he'd turned to yoga to help him cope. His training as a CIA agent had helped him with all physical aspects of evading capture for so long, but practicing yoga had helped him mentally. It had centered him, and kept him sane, so much so that he'd taken jobs as a yoga instructor in different cities all over the US, never staying too long in one place.

But in Alexandria, he'd stayed for longer than he'd planned. He should have left after his customary six weeks, but a young woman who'd attended each and every class he taught at the *Namaste Studio and Gym*, had captivated him more than he'd expected. Olivia Morikawa was a beautiful Japanese woman at least ten years his junior. Too young and too innocent for him. Yet, for the few words they exchanged during each class, he'd risked his life and nearly lost it. He could never allow that to happen again. Next time a pretty woman caught his eye, he would simply fuck her and leave town posthaste. And to think that he'd never even kissed Olivia, yet she'd had such a draw on him that he hadn't been able to bring himself to leave.

Jay brought his thoughts back to his yoga practice and started with a sun salutation, but he didn't get far. Before his eyes, everything suddenly blurred. This wasn't a nightmare, but a premonition, the very reason why he and his fellow Stargate agents were being hunted. They all had a preternatural gift. They had visions of future events. And somebody wanted to exploit this gift.

Before his eyes, a scene played out. He saw the back of a man who entered a small single-story house on a narrow street. The man glanced around the foyer, before stepping through a small archway into the open-plan living and dining area. There, he stopped, and Jay's field of vision widened, and the angle from which he watched the scene changed, so that he could now see the man's face. There was no doubt in his mind who he was. He would never forget that face. It was Smith, the man who'd captured him and nearly killed him, though Smith was obviously not his real name.

Was this Smith's home? Jay focused on the interior of the home, trying to find any clues as to where it was located. The living room was cozy and had a feminine touch. The kitchen was small, but tidy, and didn't look like anybody used it much. Maybe this was one of Smith's safehouses? He probably had several of them where he could hide out whenever he needed to.

Smith looked around and disappeared in the hallway that presumably led to the bedroom and bathroom. Smith opened a door, and behind it was an office. He entered and the vision focused on the desk. There was no computer, only a monitor and a keyboard. Next to the monitor, there were several photos. Jay jolted. The photo he now saw showed two young Japanese women laughing at the camera. He recognized one of them instantly. It was Olivia Morikawa, the woman from his yoga class in Alexandria. This was undoubtedly her home. Before Jay could grasp anything else helpful, the vision blurred, and was gone.

"Fuck!" he cursed and lost his balance. He caught himself before he could fall and widened his stance.

Olivia knew Smith. In fact, he'd entered her home as if he'd done so many times before. What was their relationship?

"You want breakfast, Jay?"

At Ace's voice coming from the open French doors, he turned. "Yeah, I need it."

Ace met his gaze. "What's going on? You're still getting dizzy? Lilly can check you out—"

"No, I'm fine. But I had a premonition just now. And Smith was in it. I think I might have a way of figuring out who and where he is."

3

Olivia felt her stomach growl and rose from her chair in front of her computer and walked into the kitchen. She opened the refrigerator and peered inside. There wasn't much, some wine, a few bottles of water, cream, condiments, and a few salad items. She wasn't exactly a great cook, but she was hungry. And a limp salad wasn't going to do it for her tonight. She'd worked hard on her book, and needed something substantial.

After locking her computer and external hard drive in the safe again, she grabbed her handbag, stuffed a couple of cloth bags into it, and left the cottage. At six o'clock, the air was humid, and the streets were still teaming with people returning from work or going out for an early dinner. Olivia didn't bother taking her car. She decided not to go to the large supermarket, which was a ten-minute drive away, but to a smaller, local market with a large deli section, where she could probably find something she only had to reheat.

She walked along the cute streets of Alexandria that led her deeper into Old Town, the touristy center of the Virginia town bordering the Potomac. She'd been very lucky to find a house so close to downtown. The rent was a little on the steep side, but it was worth it. She could walk to almost all the places she needed on a daily basis: the gym, the post office, the bank, restaurants, and shops. It was important to her, because being a writer meant she was isolated. She had no colleagues, no boss, nobody to interact with daily.

Olivia stopped in front of *Hank & Frank's*

and put her hand on the door to open it, when she heard a man call her name.

"Olivia?"

She turned on her heel and couldn't believe her eyes when she saw Jay cross the narrow cobblestone street and approach her. He looked virile in his low-riding jeans and his casual linen shirt, a small backpack thrown over one shoulder. Something was different about him though, and it took her a second to realize what it was. His head was shorn bald. When she'd last seen him, he'd had very short black hair, which had looked good on him, but she had to admit that the bald look suited him even better.

"Hi, I thought I'd recognized you," Jay said.

She finally found her voice again. "Jay, hi, we were all getting worried about you."

"Worried, why?"

"Well, you haven't shown up for your classes in two weeks, and nobody knew what had happened to you."

His brow furrowed. "But I left a voicemail for Amber letting her know that I couldn't teach." He pointed to his shoulder. "An old rotator cuff injury was playing up. I had to undergo a procedure. I'm gonna be out for another couple of weeks at least before I've got full range of motion back."

"Oh, that's good. I'm glad it's healing." Olivia let out a breath. "But it's odd, because when I asked Amber, she said she hadn't heard anything from you, and she couldn't reach you on the phone."

"Nothing against Amber," he said and leaned closer, lowering his voice to a conspiratorial whisper. "But I've seen how frazzled she gets sometimes. I bet she erased my voicemail before she even listened to it. Because if she had, she would have known that my phone was stolen, and I had to get a new number. That's why she couldn't get ahold of me."

"She'll be relieved to hear that," Olivia said with a smile. "I'll tell her."

"I'll give her a call tomorrow, so don't worry. I'll sort it out with her." Then he pointed to the store she'd been about to enter. "Am I holding you up from shopping?"

"No, no, not at all," she said quickly, not wanting him to leave now that she finally had a chance to talk to him outside of class. "I was just going to grab something for dinner. My fridge is empty."

"I was about to do the same. Just grab something I can shove in the microwave. I'm not much of a cook."

"Yeah, same here." She smiled and took a deep breath to collect all her courage. She had to ask him out now, before the moment passed. "Uh—"

"Well since we're clearly both hungry, why don't we go out to dinner together? My treat."

Her heart beat into her throat, and her stomach made an excited somersault. "Dinner, uh..." She could barely get the words out.

"Unless you're not interested. I mean, I'd understand... I uh—"

"I'm interested, definitely interested," Olivia blurted.

Jay grinned. "Yeah, me too."

At his words, she felt heat shoot into her cheeks. Oh God, she might as well have said that she wanted to sleep with him! She couldn't have been more obvious if she'd tried.

"It's still early. We might be able to get a table at the Chart House without a reservation," Jay suggested. "Do you like seafood?"

"Love it. Seafood, I mean, I love seafood." Did it show that she was nervous? Finally, she was going out to dinner with the man she'd been lusting after ever since he'd started teaching at the studio, and now she sounded like a complete idiot, not the writer who had a way with words.

"Well, then let's walk there," Jay said.

When she turned, he put his hand at the small of her back for a short moment, a gesture meant to steer her in the right direction. The touch of his hand was electrifying, and sent hot tendrils of lava into her core, just like it did whenever he used his hands to adjust her yoga poses in class.

As they walked down toward the Potomac, where the Chart House was located, Olivia tried to calm her fluttering heart. This was what she'd been waiting for ever since she'd met Jay.

"So what did you do the last two weeks since you couldn't work?" Olivia asked. She knew that men liked to talk about themselves, and it was a way for her to show him that she was interested in his life.

"Lots of physical therapy," he replied, casting her a smile. "Which gets boring day after day. I'm sure your last two weeks were more interesting than mine. I don't think you ever mentioned what you do for a living."

Surprised that Jay didn't launch into a long monologue about his life, but rather asked her questions about her own, Olivia added a few more plus-points to her mental evaluation of the handsome yoga instructor, who apparently didn't think of himself as the center of the world.

"I'm an editor," Olivia lied, regretting that she couldn't tell him what she really did. At least not yet. If things got serious, then of course she'd tell him that she was a sci-fi novelist, but so early in a relationship she couldn't reveal this secret. Relationship? She was really getting ahead of herself. What if he wasn't really interested in her?

"For a newspaper or a magazine?"

"Uh, neither. I edit novels, you know, for a publisher."

"That sounds like a fun job. You get to read novels before they're even published. You must have gotten to work on a lot of interesting books."

"Yes, I have. It's definitely a passion of mine."

"Do you work in one specific genre?"

"Yes," she said, deciding to stick to the truth as much as possible. "Sci-fi."

"Oh, I—"

"I know what you want to say... that it's something teenage boys read, but—"

He laughed. "No, I wasn't gonna say that. I was gonna say that I love reading sci-fi."

"You do? You're not just saying that?"

"No, of course not. Sci-fi is an amazing genre. It provides a great escape from all the problems in real life."

She smiled at him, pleased that he didn't dismiss her favorite genre, because it wasn't literary fiction. "I watched lots of Star Trek as a child."

"You were a Trekkie?" He chuckled. "I bet you'd look cute in one of Lieutenant Uhura's outfits."

Laughing, she gave him a light slap on his upper arm, and he snatched her hand and held it. "I guess I'd better keep your hand otherwise occupied, before you hit my injured shoulder again."

She stopped walking. "Oh, I'm so sorry, Jay, I didn't mean to hurt you."

He shook his head, still holding her hand. "You didn't, but better safe than sorry, right?" He motioned to their joined hands.

"I agree." Her heart beat excitedly. Jay was holding her hand! And it had been his move, not hers.

When they reached the restaurant, they managed to get a table on the patio, which overlooked the calm waters of the Potomac.

"I've been here a few times, mostly with my family," Olivia said after they ordered, and the waiter had brought their cocktails.

"Do they live around here, your parents and

siblings?" Jay asked, and his eyes portrayed genuine interest.

"My sister does. Grace and her fiancé live in a townhouse in D.C. But my parents moved back to Hawaii a few years ago. Dad missed the island too much."

"So your father is a native Hawaiian?"

"Yes, of Japanese descent. My mom is from Virginia. She's white."

"I'm sure there's an interesting story about how your parents met."

Olivia smiled and took a sip from her cocktail. "Mom was on vacation with her college roommates. She watched my dad surf on Waikiki beach, and I guess he swept her off her feet. It was a whirlwind romance. My sister came along less than a year later. She was actually born in Honolulu, but then Dad lost his job, and they decided to move to the mainland. Just for a while, they figured, so my grandparents could help raise us, and both my parents could work. A few years turned into twenty-five."

"They say time flies when you're happy,"

Jay said just as the food arrived. "Hmm, this looks fantastic."

As they enjoyed their food, they continued talking about family.

"And you, Jay? Do you have siblings?"

"I'm afraid not. My parents didn't stay together long enough to produce more than one child, though I did see my father regularly even after the divorce." He shrugged. "But I have lots of cousins."

She cast him a regretful smile. "I don't know what I would have done without my sister. We're very close, even though with her getting married soon, we don't spend as much time with each other as we used to." She sighed. "But I don't have any cousins. My mother and my father don't have siblings." She pointed to his dish. "How is the monkfish?"

"Excellent. Want a bite?" Jay offered, and put a small piece of the grilled fish on his fork, then leaned toward her, his hand underneath the fork so nothing could drip down. "Open up."

Olivia parted her lips and allowed him to feed her. When she took the fish from the fork and tasted it, Jay didn't immediately draw back. His face was still close to hers, almost close enough for a kiss. That thought made her hot inside again.

"Delicious," she said, but didn't solely mean the fish. She was sure that Jay's lips were even more delicious.

"Yes, I thought so myself." The way he looked at her, she wasn't sure that they were still talking about food. "How about yours? May I try your scallops?"

"Of course."

She broke eye contact and cut a piece off the huge scallops on her plate. Then she mimicked Jay's actions and leaned closer to him to feed him a piece of it. She watched him eat it with gusto, chewing quietly, then swallowing, drawing her gaze from his lips down to his throat.

"Perfect," he murmured and met her eyes. His irises seemed to take on an even richer color and now looked more green than brown. "Even better than I expected."

Olivia swallowed. "Yes, definitely."

She didn't know how she made it through

dinner and dessert, without jumping Jay's bones. He was the quintessential gentleman: polite, entertaining, and funny. His conversation was perfectly well-mannered, but the way he made eye contact with her gave his words a different meaning. Jay was flirting with her.

4

Jay looked at Olivia's luscious lips and had to force himself, for the umpteenth time, not to get lost in the fantasy of kissing her as if this was a real date and not an important mission he was on. But it was hard not to wonder what her lips would taste like, and how her body would mold itself to his if he embraced her, preferably without a stitch of clothing between them.

He'd already accomplished one task during dinner: Smith wasn't her father, because she had confirmed that her father was Japanese, and Smith was clearly white.

He could also rule out Smith as one of her uncles, because she had none. Nor any uncles-in-law either. But he couldn't stop there. Smith could easily be an acquaintance or somebody she knew professionally. However, he couldn't simply ask. For starters, he had no photo of Smith to show her, and he knew that Smith wasn't his arch enemy's real name either. And even if he had either or both of those pieces of information, he didn't know Olivia well enough to know she wouldn't run to Smith to tell him that somebody was asking questions about him. No, he had to work more clandestinely.

When Jay settled the check at the restaurant, he helped Olivia out of her chair. He didn't let go of her hand as they left the restaurant, and she didn't withdraw it.

"I'll take you home," he offered. "I'm parked a few blocks up from the store where we ran into each other." Though their meeting hadn't been accidental. He'd found out where she lived and watched the house from afar all day until she'd finally left to go grocery shopping.

"Do you mind walking me home? It's actually really close," she suggested.

"Let's walk. It's such a nice evening."

The sun had set, and the streetlamps illuminated their path. When they turned off the busy main road onto one of the quieter side streets, the streets were lit more sparingly. He kept holding Olivia's hand, liking the feel of her trusting touch. It had been a while, a long while, since he'd held hands with a woman, and he realized that he missed this innocent gesture.

"Thank you for the wonderful dinner, Jay," Olivia said.

"I'm glad I ran into you. You're great company." He wasn't lying. Talking to Olivia had been easy and fun. She was smart and kind. And she was natural. There was nothing fake about her. Whenever she'd blushed, which she did often, Jay had had to distract himself from that lovely sight and drape his napkin artfully over his lap so that she couldn't see that he was sporting a hard-on.

Like a green teenager! Clearly, he'd gone without sex for too long.

"This is where I live," Olivia said and pointed to a small cottage.

They walked to the door and stopped there. Olivia turned to him, still not letting go of his hand.

"I… uh…" She dropped her lids. "Would you…" Again, her words died.

He sensed what she wanted to say, but he hoped that she wouldn't, because if she invited him in, he wouldn't have the strength to say no.

Olivia suddenly lifted her face to him, and before he could step back, she lifted herself on her tiptoes and kissed him on the lips.

A curse escaped him.

Startled, Olivia shrank back, her shoulders touching the entrance door behind her. "I'm s—"

"Don't apologize. I want to kiss you," he said and crossed the remaining distance between them, before bracing one hand next to her head against the door. "But are you sure you want this? Because if we kiss, I'm not going to be able to keep my hands off you. It was hard enough to keep my distance during class."

"Why would you want to keep your distance when you want to kiss me?"

"I'm quite a bit older than you. And I'm not exactly boyfriend material." That was true, but it wasn't the entire truth. He didn't want to use her. In order to plant surveillance equipment in her house, he didn't need to sleep with her. He could simply sneak in at a later time when she was out, and be done with it.

"I don't care if you're boyfriend material or not, Jay." She put her hands on his hips and pulled him toward her, until his groin pressed against her stomach.

A startled gasp escaped Olivia's lips. "Ohh."

"Yeah, I'm hard." He knew she could feel him. "And if you invite me into your house tonight, we both know what'll happen. So, please tell me to go home and sleep in my own bed."

Olivia suddenly smirked and lifted one hand to his nape. "No, you're not going anywhere tonight but my bed." She slanted her lips over his.

"Ah, fuck it," he cursed and took what she

offered him, kissing her mouth hungrily for a few seconds, before he ripped his lips from hers. "Keys?"

She pulled her keys from her purse, and he took them and put them in the lock, when Olivia kissed him again and slid her palm over the bulge in his jeans. He nearly leapt out of his shoes, the touch jolting him, and making him realize that the desire he felt for Olivia wouldn't be stilled by only one fuck in just one night.

Somehow, he managed to unlock the door and slam it shut behind them. He dropped his backpack on the floor, where it landed next to Olivia's handbag. In the darkness of the foyer, he pressed her against the door and captured her lips again, dueled with her tongue, and explored her, while he ground his cock against her stomach.

He knew she was twenty-eight years old, so what they were doing was definitely legal, but everything about Olivia screamed innocent. Yet, here he was, practically mauling her, and ready to fuck her against the door. He had to slow down, or she would change her mind and realize that having invited him in was more than she'd bargained for.

Breathing heavily, Jay severed the kiss. "Olivia, are you sure about this?"

"Make love to me," she answered without hesitation.

"Where's your bedroom?"

She took his hand and led him into the house, through the living room into a short hallway with three doors, two of them open. Olivia led him into the room on the left and flipped a light switch. The low light of the bedside lamps bathed the room in a soft glow. A queen-size bed with crisp white sheets dominated the small room. With his foot, Jay kicked the door shut, before pulling Olivia back into his arms.

Olivia was already busying herself by tugging on his shirt, unbuttoning it hastily. He took her hands in his, stilling them.

"Slow down," he murmured. "We've got all night. Unless you're planning on kicking me to the curb the moment you climax."

She suddenly froze. Had he been too presumptuous in assuming she'd allow him to stay the night? Wasn't that what women wanted?

"I'm sorry. Did I say something wrong?"

Olivia shook her head, then dropped her gaze. "No, of course not. It's just..."

"What is it?"

"I don't normally... I mean... it's really difficult for me... uhm..."

Jay put his fingers under her chin and tipped her face up so he could look into her eyes. "Whatever it is, you can tell me."

She drew in a breath. "I don't normally climax during sex. I mean, it doesn't matter, and—"

He put a finger on her lips. "Tonight will be different." He'd make sure of that. The least he could do was to give her pleasure. "Just relax, and I'll take care of you. Let me undress you."

Slowly, he began to lower the zipper of her colorful summer dress until he could slide the straps down her shoulders, so the soft fabric slid down her torso. Underneath, she wore a bra that matched her skin color. Her breasts were small, but her nipples already pressed through the thin fabric, attesting to her arousal. Gently, he pulled the dress over her slim hips until she stepped out of it. Her panties were the same color and fabric as her bra. Jay picked up the dress and laid it over a nearby chair, then bent down and helped her take off her sandals, before he rose again.

He stepped back, kicked off his shoes and unbuttoned his linen shirt, then shrugged out of it, and tossed it on the chair too. When he put his hands on the waistband of his jeans, he heard Olivia inhale a breath. He met her gaze, then continued opening the button. When he lowered the zipper, Olivia's gaze focused on his groin, and she licked her lower lip.

The gesture was so sexy, yet so innocent that he almost came right there and then. He had to clench his jaw to restrain himself, before he could take off his jeans and toss them aside. He quickly took off his socks, before he straightened again and faced Olivia, now only wearing his boxer briefs. The black fabric stretched, his cock beneath it hard and heavy.

"You're beautiful," she murmured and

reached out to him, placing her hand on his chest to caress the hard ridges.

"Compared to you, I'm Quasimodo," he said lightheartedly.

A smile played around her lips, and he noticed her relax. It was evident that this was new for her, that she didn't often take guys home with her to have casual sex. If ever.

Jay pulled her into his arms and kissed her gently, his lips not demanding, but coaxing, allowing her to go at her own speed. Olivia parted her lips, and her tongue darted out. He angled his head to allow her better access, and she swept her tongue into his mouth and licked against his. At the contact, a spear of fire charged through his core, and he couldn't help himself but press Olivia firmer against his body, his cock now rubbing against her stomach, enjoying the softness cradling him.

He slid his hands to the clasp of her bra and unhooked it. She let out a soft gasp, before intensifying the kiss and pressing her breasts firmer against him. He could feel her hard nipples rub against his chest.

Without haste, he slipped the straps of her

bra over her shoulders and stepped back a little so he could free her from it completely. When the bra fell to the ground, he pulled her back against him and felt her breasts caress his chest. A moan escaped him, and he lifted Olivia up in his arms and lowered her onto the bed, joining her, his lips still on hers. He didn't roll over her, not yet. Instead, he loosened their embrace so he could touch her breasts. He took one of her globes into his hand, kneading it and playing with the stiff bud, rolling it between his thumb and index finger.

Olivia moaned and arched her back, pressing her breast into his palm. He released her lips and looked at her. Her face was glistening, her eyes shining back at him as if in a daze.

"Let me take care of you now," he murmured and dipped his head to her breasts. He licked first one then the other nipple, before he closed his lips around one of them, and started sucking and licking her beautiful flesh, while he kneaded the other one.

Olivia sighed and moaned, one hand now clutching the duvet and holding on to it for dear life. Her other hand wandered to his nape and caressed him there. The touch sent a jolt through his body and straight to his cock. Involuntarily, he swung one leg between her thighs, and rubbed his cock against her leg.

"You feel so good," she said on a raspy breath.

He let her nipple pop from his mouth. "You feel even better." Then he slid down on her body and freed her from her panties. He spread her legs wider, before settling in between her thighs, his head at her groin.

"Jay, what are you—"

He angled her legs to expose her sex to him, silencing her question. Her pink flesh was beautiful, soft, and glistening with her juices. "Beautiful," he murmured, then cast a glance up to her face and saw that she looked at him in utter amazement. "I'd like to make you come with my mouth, baby, if you don't mind."

"Mind?" Her chest heaved, and her cheeks flushed even more.

Jay licked over her warm cleft, gathering her juices on his tongue, and saw how Olivia's head dropped back on the pillow.

"Hmm, you taste delicious. Had I known, I wouldn't have ordered dessert."

Olivia let out a gasp. "You're unreal."

"Trust me, I'm real." He sank his lips onto her pussy, and began to lick her in earnest, while he slid his palms underneath her ass to tilt her up, so he could feast on her. He'd always loved eating pussy, but in the last few years, he hadn't met a woman he wanted to perform this intimate act on.

Beneath him, Olivia moaned, both hands now clutching the duvet, her hips moving, her sex releasing more juices. He used one hand to gain better access to her clit. The tiny organ was swollen. He licked over it gently at first, then with more pressure. Olivia let out a startled cry.

"Like that?" he asked.

"Oh yes, Jay, please, do it again."

He repeated the action, eliciting another moan from her. She rubbed herself against his tongue, her hips now moving in a faster tempo. He adjusted his rhythm and speed to hers and licked her center of pleasure, drawing tiny circles around the organ, while he ran one finger along her slit. On her next moan, he thrust his finger into her channel. His lips around her clit, he pressed them together tightly. Beneath him, Olivia shuddered. He felt her climax physically as her interior muscles spasmed around his finger multiple times, until the waves ebbed. When she stilled, he pulled his finger from her and released her clit.

Slowly, he moved up her body and pulled her into his arms. "See? You do climax during sex."

"Because of what you did. Can I do the same to you?"

She slid her hand to his boxer briefs and laid her palm over the bulge there.

Jay put his hand on hers. "I didn't do this so you'd reciprocate with a blow job. I did this because I wanted to lick your pussy and make you come."

"What if I want to suck your cock? Would you say no?"

5

Olivia stared into Jay's eyes, surprise flickering in them.

"Are you sure you want that?" he asked.

She squeezed his cock, loving how it twitched under her touch. She'd never felt so satisfied from sex, and she wanted Jay to feel the same way.

"Take them off."

"Yes, ma'am," he said as if he were in the military, and she his commanding officer.

When he took off his black boxer briefs, she laid eyes on his cock for the first time. She'd felt that he was big, but now she saw the full extent of it. He was enormous—and beautiful. His cock was hard, and pre-cum was already seeping from the tiny hole on its tip. Thick veins snaked around his shaft, and when she wrapped her palm around him, she felt the velvety soft skin covering the steel-hard rod. She sucked in a breath. She wanted to feel him inside her. He would stretch her, would barely fit, but she wanted to feel him thrust into her nevertheless.

"Lie down on your back," she ordered, and he complied.

She swept her eyes over his body. He was muscular where it counted and lean everywhere else. His hips were narrow, and there was barely any hair on his chest. His cock stood erect amidst a bed of dark curls. Olivia slid between his spread thighs and leaned down. She dipped her head to his cock, her tongue already darting out to lick him, when she heard him inhale sharply.

"Fuck!" he hissed.

She swept her lids up and caught his gaze. His eyes seemed to blaze with lust, and at the sight, a feeling of power surged inside her. It struck her right then: Jay would surrender to her, just like she'd surrendered to him. She'd never particularly enjoyed giving a guy a blow job, but what she saw in Jay's eyes made her excited about taking his cock into her mouth and pleasuring him until he begged her to stop.

Olivia licked over the bulbous tip of his shaft and tasted the salty drops covering the crown. She inhaled his masculine scent and wrapped her lips around the tip of his erection, then licked it to lubricate it, before she put her hand around the base and took him into her mouth as deep as she could.

Jay groaned as if in pain and gripped her shoulders. "Fuck, Olivia! Are you trying to make me spill in under two seconds?"

She didn't bother replying, but slowly lifted her head to release part of his cock. She kept its tip in her mouth and sucked, her cheeks hollowing with the motion.

"Fuck, you're good!" he rasped.

His comment pleased her, and she slid down on him again. This time she tried to loosen her jaw so she could take him deeper.

With her free hand she gripped his balls and squeezed the tight sac gently. Jay's cock spasmed in her mouth, and he moaned. But he didn't make her withdraw, didn't demand she let go of his balls. Instead, he thrust his hips up, demanding she move up and down on him. She followed his unspoken command, and withdrew, then descended again. Her tempo increased, and she now moved her hand around his root in the same rhythm and speed.

Jay's hands on her shoulders moved to the back of her head, guiding her, not forcing her. She liked that, because it meant he accepted that she was in charge. For the first time during sex with a man, she felt that she was the dominant partner, that she was the one who called the shots. It didn't matter that Jay was so much bigger and stronger than her, because he was surrendering his power to her.

"Baby," he suddenly called out. "You've gotta stop, or I'll come."

She let his cock plop from her mouth and looked up at him. "I thought that was the point."

He chuckled. "It is, but I'd rather come inside your pussy."

Olivia smiled at him and crawled up.

"How about you ride me?" Jay asked. "You'll be in control."

"I like that." She bent across to the nightstand and opened the top drawer. She pulled a condom from it and ripped the package open, ready to roll it over Jay's cock.

"I'd better do that myself," he said and took the condom from her hand. "I'm afraid if you do it, I'll climax immediately."

"Are you always that easily aroused?"

He started rolling the condom over his cock and tossed her a look. "Do you always look so sexy?"

He thought her sexy? She'd never seen herself as sexy. Pretty, yes, but more in a nice-girl kind of way.

"God, you don't even know how hot you are, do you?" he asked and pulled her on top of him, so her legs dropped to either side of his hips.

He adjusted his cock to line it up with her pussy, then met her eyes. "Take me inside you when you're ready. Take all the time you need so it won't hurt. I might be a little big."

"A little big?" She shook her head laughing. "I'd call it huge." Slowly, she lowered herself onto him, his cock parting her nether lips. She felt how her muscles stretched, and so far only the bulbous head of his cock was inside her. "Make that enormous," she corrected herself.

She saw him close his eyes and suck in a breath. "Fuck, you're tight." He pulled his lower lip between his teeth and exhaled slowly. She found the sight of him trying to fight the urge to come more than just a little erotic. She found it intoxicating, so much so that she felt herself get even wetter, and knew she was ready to take more of him. She lowered herself an inch, then another. Now, she could finally bear down on him until he was submerged in her to the hilt.

"Fuck!" Jay let out.

"I think I love enormous," she said on a breath and lowered her head to his to kiss him. "I love how you fill me completely."

He put one hand on her nape, holding her close to him, before she felt his other hand on her sex, touching her clitoris. "Now ride me, baby, and I'll make sure we'll come together this time."

He began caressing her clit.

"Is that why you suggested I ride you?"

"Yes, because it means I can use my fingers to touch your clit and make you come."

Olivia sat up straight and began to move. She started in a slow rhythm, but with every second, her tempo increased, and they were both panting. Jay's ministrations to her clit heightened her arousal, and she wondered for a split-second why none of her previous boyfriends had ever employed that technique to make her climax. Yet Jay, a man who barely knew her, knew instinctively how to pleasure her.

The need to come rose inside her, and she could feel it already, could sense the approach of her orgasm. She threw her head back and impaled herself harder and faster on Jay's cock, and with his free hand on her hip, he encouraged her to ride him with more fervor, while his fingers on her clit played her as if she were an instrument and he a talented musician.

"Jay! Oh, God! Jay, I'm coming!"

"Yes!" he cried out.

A moment later, she climaxed and felt Jay's cock spasm inside her. But he didn't stop, didn't withdraw from her. Instead, he moved, and an instant later, she found herself with her back on the bed, Jay above her, thrusting into her hard and deep.

"Fuck, Olivia!" he cursed, before his movements became slower and he finally stilled, braced above her on his elbows and knees.

He gazed into her eyes. "I don't think I've ever come so hard." He pressed a gentle kiss on her lips.

Olivia put her hand on the back of his bald head and smiled at him. "I've never come like this at all. How did you know what I needed?"

"I just did what I thought you'd enjoy." He rolled off her and rid himself of the condom, then pulled her back into his arms. "Is it okay if I stay the night?"

Her heart warmed at the knowledge that he

wasn't the type of man who left the moment he'd gotten what he wanted. Jay was the sensitive kind, the kind of man she'd been hoping to find all her life.

"I've wanted this ever since you started teaching at *Namaste*."

Jay chuckled. "That's a yes then, I guess."

She snuggled against him, knowing she didn't have to give him an answer, because he already knew what she wanted.

6

It was shortly before 2 a.m. when Jay woke like he'd planned. Olivia was sleeping peacefully. He peeled himself out of her arms and waited for a moment, making sure the action hadn't woken her, but she continued sleeping. Quietly, and still naked, he got out of bed and walked to the door. He opened it without making a sound, then slipped outside and walked to the foyer, where he'd dropped his backpack earlier. He didn't switch on any lights. The light shining in from the streetlamp outside was sufficient for what he needed to do. The CIA had trained him well. And Fox had supplied him with the equipment he needed. All he had to do was to install it.

He removed the tiny surveillance devices from an inner pouch of his backpack and went to work. He installed the first device in the foyer to capture anybody entering and leaving the cottage. Two more devices he positioned in the living room and attached kitchen area, one hidden inside a heating vent, the other on a high shelf with decorative plates that, judging by the dust around them, had never been used or moved.

He walked back to the corridor and listened for any sounds from the bedroom, but it was quiet in there. He marched into the other room, an office, and looked for a convenient place to hide the device. He decided on installing it on the wall where Olivia had set up her computer workstation, though he couldn't see a laptop, only a large monitor and external keyboard. Above the large screen was an abstract wall clock made of metal and wire mesh. It reminded him of a clock the famous Salvador Dali had painted. He managed to hide the camera and listening device within the mesh and was confident that nobody would spot it.

He contemplated whether to install another one in Olivia's bedroom, but decided against it. If she really had something to do with Smith, he doubted that Olivia would invite him into her bedroom. She wasn't that kind of woman. Yes, she'd invited him, but he was pretty sure she'd had a crush on him since they'd met and she wasn't somebody who dated several men at the same time. Jay too, had had a crush on her ever since he'd first laid eyes on her. But he'd suppressed his desire for fear of dragging her into his fucked-up life.

He sighed. Fuck! Why had he slept with her? Why couldn't he have simply broken in when she wasn't home? It would have been so easy. Yet he hadn't been able to resist seeing her, even though he knew what it would lead to. What it *had* led to. Making love to her had been more amazing than he could have ever imagined. Which was also the reason why he felt a pang of guilt now.

He should disappear right now, leave while

Olivia was still sleeping, but he couldn't do that to her. She would feel betrayed, and he didn't want to hurt her. However, he had no idea how to let her down easily, without her feeling that he'd taken advantage of her. But eventually he would have to do just that, because he couldn't stay in Alexandria. His place here was compromised.

Jay suddenly heard a sound coming from the bedroom. He quickly opened the door and snuck inside.

"Jay?"

"I'm here."

"Are you leaving?"

He heard the panic in her voice, and quickly slid under the covers. "I just needed to drink some water. I didn't mean to wake you."

She snuggled into his arms, and the feel of her soft curves pressing against his body aroused him. He kissed her neck and shoulder and she sighed in a way that told him that she wouldn't go back to sleep right away. Neither would he. Not with the hard-on he was sporting already. He reached toward the bedside table and snatched a condom from it. He quickly rolled it over his erection and spooned her again.

"Tell me you're not sore," he whispered into Olivia's ear.

"Ohh," she murmured and pressed her sweet ass against his groin. "I'm not sore at all."

He reached between her legs and found her pussy wet. "Thank God." Then he aligned his cock with her sex and thrust into her from behind.

"Ohh!" Olivia cried out.

Jay froze. "Too hard?"

"No." She began to move. "I like it."

This time, their coupling was slower and gentler. They were both more relaxed and were getting to know each other's bodies. He took his time with her, made sure she got what she needed so she would at least look back on this night as a satisfying one. A pleasant memory. When they climaxed together, Jay held her in his arms until she fell asleep again, before pulling out of her warm cave, still semi-hard.

It took him a long time to fall asleep, but it was a peaceful sleep this time. For the first time since his fellow Stargate agents had rescued him, his sleep wasn't haunted by the recollections of what Smith had done to him.

When he woke around 7a.m., Olivia was still asleep. He took a shower and got dressed, then went into the kitchen and checked the refrigerator and cupboards. He found coffee, some cream and not much else. He was about to make coffee, when he heard the bedroom door and the sound of bare feet on the old hardwood floor.

He turned and saw Olivia walk toward him, dressed in a large white T-shirt. She smiled at him. "You're still here."

"I was gonna make us breakfast, but your fridge is pretty empty."

"Yeah, sorry. I was gonna go shopping last night, but then a handsome man whisked me off to dinner, and I didn't get a chance to buy groceries."

He chuckled. Damn, she looked cute in the morning. "So it's my fault then? Fair enough. How about I take you out for breakfast?" At least then he wouldn't drag her back to bed.

Olivia beamed. "Give me fifteen minutes, and I'll be ready."

She wasn't joking. It truly took her only fifteen minutes to shower and get ready. He'd never met a woman who was so uncomplicated.

At a cozy little breakfast place two blocks from Olivia's cottage, they ordered coffee and croissants, and sat at a tiny bistro table in the morning sun. It felt like he was living somebody else's life. The life of somebody who was happy and carefree. A life that didn't belong to him. He knew it wouldn't last. His enemies were on his heels, and he had no right to drag Olivia into this.

He shouldn't even be here at this coffee shop, where any passerby could recognize him and report to Smith that he was still in the area.

"I had a really nice time last night," Jay said, leaning closer to Olivia.

She lifted her lids and looked into his eyes. "I did too. I'm so glad I ran into you." Then she let out a breath. "I was wondering... I mean, I know this might come out of left field...but..." She hesitated.

He kissed her on the cheek and inhaled her sweet scent. "What?"

"Well, Grace, my sister, is getting married this weekend, and I don't have a date for the wedding. I wondered if maybe you wanted to come with me."

She'd blurted out the words, and Jay realized that she was using all her courage to make this suggestion.

Fuck! As much as he would have liked to accompany her to a wedding, there was no way he could do that. At an event like that, the chance that somebody connected to Smith would recognize him was even higher than sitting in this café.

"Uhm," he said, trying to find a way to let her down without hurting her. "I'm not really the wedding kind of guy. I mean, you don't really know me, and your family will be there, and..."

"I get it," she said, and the smile she gave him looked forced. "It's okay. I just thought I'd ask."

"If I could come with you, I would," Jay said and put his fingers under her chin, making her look at him. "It's just that there's a lot going on in my life right now." He pressed a kiss to her lips and felt like a total jerk. Olivia deserved a real boyfriend, a man who could commit to her, not a man who used her to get information on Smith.

He needed to get out of here before he made things even worse.

"It's getting late," he said. "I need to get to my physical therapy appointment."

"Oh, sure. Are you doing anything later? Maybe we could meet up."

"Wish I could, but I've got lots of errands to run. Can I call you?"

"Sure." She pulled out her cell phone and unlocked it. "Give me your number, so I can send you mine."

Damn, she was smart. He had no choice but to give her the number of the burner Fox had given him to communicate with the other ex-Stargate agents. When his cell phone pinged, he said, "Got it."

He'd have to get rid of the SIM card later

and exchange it for another one to make sure he couldn't be traced should the number fall into Smith's hands. He regretted having to do this, but his life and that of the other agents was on the line. And he couldn't risk lives because he had a crush on a beautiful girl. Ah, fuck, who was he kidding? It wasn't just a crush. He'd been slowly falling for Olivia ever since he'd first adjusted her hips in her Downward Dog pose in class. Making love to her had cemented the fact that this was no fleeting crush.

But he couldn't act on his feelings, no matter how much it hurt to let Olivia go.

7

"Look who's back," Fox announced as Jay entered the computer room in Ace's mansion. "Must've been a good night."

The room was equipped with the latest technology, and according to Fox, the gray color the room was painted with prevented any enemy from eavesdropping on them, should they ever find out where they were holed up.

Fox wasn't alone. In fact, the entire gang was assembled. Michelle was sitting next to Fox, typing away on a keyboard, while Ace and Yankee were hunched over a large map that was spread out on the biggest desk in the room. Phoebe and Lilly were going through stacks of printouts and comparing them to other stacks of paper.

"Hey, guys," Jay said.

Everybody greeted him.

Ace motioned to a computer monitor in one corner. "We're piping the cameras and sound recordings of Olivia's house right into that PC. It's recording everything. Good job."

"Yeah," Fox added, "the cameras are placed perfectly. We'll see if Smith shows up there like in your premonition. And if she talks to him on the phone, we'll be able to record at least her side of the conversation."

Jay nodded, though he didn't feel very proud about what he'd done. "That's good."

"Hey, Tiger," Fox said. "Didn't I give you five devices to install? Must've miscounted."

"You didn't. I had a fifth one, but I decided not to bug her bedroom."

"Why not? What if Smith is her lover?" Fox asked.

"You know, pillow talk and all," Yankee added.

"He's not her lover," Jay said.

"How would you know that? Sure, there's an age difference, but maybe he's her sugar daddy," Fox insisted.

"He's not!" Jay ground out, getting in Fox's face, glaring at him.

Fox let out a breath. "And you know that because you spent one night with her? Come on."

"Nick!" Michelle put her hand on Fox's arm. "Don't! It's none of your business, or would you like me to remind you that you thought you could keep emotions out of it when you slept with me to get info on Smith, and that you failed just as miserably as Tiger?"

Jay didn't know whether he should be grateful to Michelle for reigning in her boyfriend or be annoyed that she'd seen right through him.

"Sorry, Jay," Michelle said. "But I saw on the recording this morning how you looked at her. Kinda hard to miss."

Ah, fuck! Now everybody knew his business, and they were all staring at him. He glared back at them. "I'm doing what I'm supposed to be doing: use her to find Smith. End of story. It doesn't matter that I fucked her, okay? She's a means to an end."

Who was he kidding? Not even he believed that.

"We have to get to Smith, and Olivia is our only lead so far. Or have you found a better one?" Jay snapped.

Ace rose, though he spoke in a calm voice. "Nothing yet. We're still working on going through traffic cameras and any cameras at train and Metro stations in the vicinity of the warehouse we blew up, but so far, his face hasn't shown up anywhere." He pointed to Lilly. "Lilly is cross-referencing every car registration with the driver's licenses of the owners to see if she recognizes his face. Yankee has been doing the same."

"Yeah, the problem is," Fox interjected, "that we have to do it all manually. If we had an actual picture of Smith, we could run it through facial recognition. But we don't have one."

Jay took a long breath, calming himself. He knew everybody was doing their best, working tirelessly to find Smith and whomever he worked for. They all had the same goal.

"I'm just a bit worn out," Jay admitted.

"How's your head?" Lilly asked, concerned, and rose from her chair. "Still getting headaches?" She was a doctor, a medical researcher actually, but had gone into hiding with Yankee after Smith had targeted her for elimination. She and Yankee now lived at Ace's mansion, just like Jay.

"Not as much anymore, thanks."

"If you want me to give you something for it..." Lilly offered.

"I'm good. I don't want to be drugged." Smith had drugged him, and he'd felt helpless. He never wanted to feel like that again. He'd rather feel pain. "I need to keep a clear head." He turned to Ace. "What do you want me to work on?"

"How about a quick run-down of what you've found out about Olivia Morikawa so far, and how she could be connected to Smith?" Ace asked.

Jay nodded. "She comes from a small family. Her father is from Hawaii. Japanese, which means Smith isn't her father, nor an uncle, because we know that Smith is white and in his fifties or early sixties." Which was a huge relief. Because having feelings for his arch enemy's daughter would be the worst thing that could happen to him. "Neither her mother nor her father have siblings. That also means there are no cousins. I'm pretty certain that she's not related to Smith. That leaves friends, acquaintances, and any professional connections."

"Is it possible that she works for him?" Ace asked.

"I doubt it. She's an editor for a publisher in the sci-fi genre. I'm gonna have to dig a little deeper on that, but it shouldn't be too hard to figure out who she works for. There must be a W-2 or some other tax forms that show who this publisher is."

"You didn't ask her the name of her employer?" Ace asked.

"It didn't come up. I didn't wanna be too obvious and sound like I was giving her the third degree."

"All right. Friends? Acquaintances?"

Jay pointed to the computer with the grid of camera angles showing the inside of Olivia's cottage. "That's where the bugs will come in handy. We'll figure out who visits her, and whom she talks with on the phone. I got her cell number, too." He turned to Fox. "Fox, can you get her phone bills to see whom she speaks to regularly?"

"Sure thing."

Jay pulled out his cell phone and checked the number from which Olivia had called him in the café. "Her number is 202-555-0977."

"Got it."

"Oh, and I need a new SIM card. Can't use this number anymore. Olivia knows it."

Fox raised an eyebrow. Judging by his facial expression, Fox was probably thinking that he was an amateur, but Fox had enough sense not to voice his thoughts. "Give it to me. I'll put a new one in."

"Thanks, appreciate it." Jay handed him his cell phone. Then he looked back at Ace. "So, what next?"

Ace walked toward him. "You could give me a hand with something outside."

"Sure." Whatever it was, it was better than doing nothing and thinking back to his night with Olivia. Because the more he thought about her, the guiltier he felt.

They left the computer room and closed the door behind them. Ace led them to a smaller room, which Jay knew was Ace's private office.

"I thought you wanted me to help you with something outside."

Ace grimaced. "I wanted to talk to you alone. Come."

Jay entered the small office with the mahogany wood paneling and the heavy desk and looked around. "Was this Sheppard's?"

Henry Sheppard, the director of the top-secret Stargate program at the CIA, had adopted Scott Thompson at age eleven, and years later, Sheppard had given him the code name Ace. Ace became the first agent in the program Sheppard spearheaded until his untimely death more than three years earlier.

Ace shook his head. "My father never worked at home. When he came home, it was always just the two of us, talking, playing..."

"So he was a good father then?"

"The best. He understood me, and I understood him."

"You were lucky. I wish somebody had understood my gift early on." Instead, he'd thought himself a freak of nature.

"I was lucky, yes. But we're not here to talk about me. How are you really, Jay?"

Surprised that Ace addressed him by his given name rather than his code name, Jay stared at him for a few seconds, before he had an answer to this seemingly mundane question.

"The headaches are getting better."

"How about the nightmares?"

Jay let out a gasp. "How—"

"Phoebe," Ace said. "The farther along in the pregnancy she gets, the worse she sleeps. She heard you when she walked past your room. She wasn't prying, trust me, but she's worried about you. So am I."

"I'm fine." Yeah, that was another big, fat lie.

"We both know you're not. You barely escaped with your life. Nobody would judge you if you took some time for yourself to recover fully. We have everything in hand."

"Not doing anything makes it worse. What Smith did to me was worse than any physical torture I've ever endured. He tried to take my thoughts from me, my brain, the very thing that defines me. Without my mind, I'm nothing. Without my premonitions, I'm not complete, I'm not me. You must understand that. And he was trying to take it away to build a fucking quantum computer to do God-knows what awful things."

Ace nodded, his expression serious. "And we'll get him for that. Eventually. Listen, you've been through more than the rest of us, so don't take this the wrong way, but the machine he used to try and scan your brain waves might have altered your mind."

"What are you saying?"

Ace sighed. "I'm just saying, maybe your judgment is off right now. Maybe you need to step back to see the bigger picture."

"Why don't you come right out with it, huh? Why don't you tell me to my face that you don't approve that I fucked Olivia? That for once in my life I took what I wanted without giving a damn about the consequences? I don't see you living like a monk. So you know what, Ace? Fuck you!"

"I was afraid you'd say that," Ace said calmly.

"What the fuck?"

All of a sudden, Ace chuckled. "Guess Michelle was right. You like Olivia."

Jay already opened his mouth to tell Ace to shove his opinions where the sun didn't shine, but his fellow Stargate agent stopped him.

"Hey, I'm not blaming you. I just hope for your own sake that it turns out that Olivia has nothing to do with the evil things Smith is behind. Or if she does that you can get her to switch sides. Now, go and rest for a few hours. We'll take turns watching the live feed from Olivia's house. You can take over later."

Jay took a long breath, before he nodded. "All right." Maybe after a few hours of rest he would feel better, though he doubted that the guilt he felt about using Olivia would dissipate no matter how long he rested.

8

As Ace had requested, Jay rested, which in his case meant he practiced yoga out in the backyard and meditated. Then he went for a jog, but since he couldn't leave the property for fear of being recognized, he stayed within the walls of the property and ran around the mansion, before using the indoor stairs as a way to exercise. Sweating, he went back to his room, undressed and showered, and dressed in clean clothes, before he joined several of the others for a late afternoon meal in the large kitchen, during which everybody came and went at their leisure. It was rare that they all sat together for a meal at the same time. Somebody was always manning the computers, just in case anything came up that had to be acted upon without delay.

Feeling that his mind was a little clearer now, he went into the computer room, eager to contribute to the search for the elusive Mr. Smith.

His three Stargate colleagues stood around the computer that showed the surveillance footage of Olivia's cottage. Why the fuck were they gaping at the computer screen? Were they watching her get undressed?

Annoyance churned up in him as he approached. "What's going on?"

All three turned around and stared at him, nobody saying a word. He bridged the distance to the monitor and looked at the screen. He spotted Olivia sitting in her office, fully dressed, and typing on the keyboard. There was nothing going on in her cottage. She had no visitors. So why were Ace, Fox, and Yankee looking so glum?

"Play it back, Fox, and turn up the volume," Ace said.

Fox made a few keystrokes, and the window showing Olivia's office now filled the entire screen. Fox hit the play button.

Olivia's cell phone rang. She looked at it, picked it up, and pressed it to her ear.

"I couldn't reach you earlier."

There was a short pause, during which the other person spoke, but Jay couldn't hear that side of the conversation, only Olivia's replies.

"Like I said, I need to come up with something good, before it goes sideways... no, that's too early... I mean we barely know at this point what skeletons he's got in the closet... I think it's only fair to reveal them before..."

There was a longer pause, during which Jay held his breath. Who was she talking about?

"No, I can't kill him yet. Way too early."

"Fuck!" Jay cursed and exchanged a look with his fellow agents, who looked just as shocked as he felt. But he had no time to digest the news, because Olivia continued.

"Besides, I haven't figured out the manner of death yet. Belladonna gets old, and it doesn't really fit either. And daggers are messy..." Then she laughed unexpectedly.

"Yeah, that would be gory. But I've done that too often already. I want something new, something fresh. I'm just not feeling it right now, you know?" She paused again. "And before I forget it, there's still the issue with the second lover. I'm gonna have to resolve that before I can get rid of him." She shook her head. "No, it has to be in a way that he won't see it coming, nor anybody else for that matter. Would you please put your thinking cap on for me? I'm just a little tired today. Thanks, okay, yeah, bye."

Olivia disconnected the call and went back to typing happily on her keyboard as if she hadn't just been planning somebody's murder. And if his suspicion was right, *his* murder.

Fox paused the recording, and for a few seconds, nobody said anything. Only the humming of the computers and the air conditioning could be heard in the room.

"She's planning to kill me," Jay said, the blood freezing in his veins. How could he have been so wrong about her?

"Well, you can't know that for sure," Fox

said with a shrug. "She didn't mention your name."

"Would you if you were on an unsecured line?" Jay asked.

"No, but then I wouldn't discuss murder on a cell phone either," Fox shot back.

"She doesn't really strike me as a cold-blooded assassin," Yankee added. "Though if she is, it's a bloody good disguise. She's got the innocent librarian type down pat."

"Let's not draw hasty conclusions," Ace said. "Perhaps there's an innocent explanation for this conversation. How about we first find out who she was talking to. Fox?"

"Might take a while, since the call only just happened. I'll have to hack into the current logs of her carrier. That's a little more involved than her old phone bills."

"Do that," Jay said, appreciating Ace's suggestion. He didn't want to believe that Olivia wanted him dead. But what other conclusion could he draw from the things she'd said on the phone? And even if she wasn't planning *his* murder, but somebody else's, it would still mean the same, namely that Olivia was a killer. And he couldn't accept that.

"I have to go see her." The words were out before he even realized that he'd made the decision to go into the lion's den, or in this case, the lioness's den.

"Are you fucking crazy?" Yankee asked. "Didn't you just say yourself that she's planning to kill you?"

"She also said that she hasn't figured out the manner of death yet, so I figure I'm safe for tonight," Jay hedged.

"Unless she improvises," Fox interrupted.

"Aren't you supposed to hack into her cell records?" Jay barked.

Fox lifted his hands in surrender. "Don't say I didn't warn you." He marched to his workstation.

"Are you sure about this, Tiger?" Ace asked, casting him a long hard look.

"I'll go in armed."

Ace scoffed. "And what are you gonna say when you see her? You can't just ask her point blank."

"I'll think of something." With a glance at Fox he added, "Maybe I'll improvise."

Fox flipped him the bird. "Go get yourself killed. I'll text you the moment I know who she was talking to."

An hour later, Jay left the mansion and made his way to Alexandria, taking all precautions possible in case somebody tried to tail him somewhere on the way. He changed transportation several times to make sure nobody was following him, and he checked out the area around Olivia's cottage to be sure that nobody lay in wait outside. Ace had confirmed over the phone that nobody had entered or left Olivia's house since she'd made the phone call earlier.

He couldn't stall any longer. From outside, he saw that there was still light in Olivia's office, though when he looked in through the window, he didn't see her. Jay walked around to the front door, and pressed the doorbell. He heard the soft chime sounding inside the house. Footsteps came closer a moment later, and then the light under the tiny portico where Jay stood was switched on.

A second later, the door opened, and Olivia looked at him, clearly stunned. Then a wide smile spread on her face as she reached for him.

"Why didn't you call that you were coming over?" she asked and motioned to her clothing. She wore a nightgown and a bathrobe over it. "I would have gotten dressed." She blushed.

Would a murderess really blush like Olivia? Damn, he hoped not.

"If I'm disturbing you, I can leave. I just thought maybe..."

She pulled him inside, her arms already snaking around him, while he kicked the door shut behind him and sank his mouth onto her inviting lips. She tasted of mint and innocence, and he couldn't resist the open invitation, whether it came from a killer or not. His mouth still claiming hers, he pressed her with her back against the wall and shoved his hands underneath her bathrobe to roam her body, all the way up and down her back, then her front. He was relieved to find that she didn't have any weapons on her. But he'd also felt that she wasn't wearing panties under her thin nightgown that didn't even reach halfway to her knees. He pulled the fabric up and slid his hand between her legs. Wetness and warmth greeted him when he touched her there.

Olivia moaned into his mouth, her chest heaving, her pelvis rocking against his hand, asking for more. Fuck! How could she want him like this yet also want to kill him? It made no sense. The woman in his arms was ready to surrender to him after just one kiss. How could she be a stone-cold killer? Nothing about Olivia was cold-blooded. This wasn't a woman who was in control of anything right now. On the contrary. In the dark of the foyer, she was at his mercy. If he wanted to, he could fuck her right here, against the wall. And she wouldn't protest. Because the woman now rubbing herself against his fingers, and releasing moans of pleasure, was in the throes of lust, only out for one thing: to climax in his arms.

He ripped his lips from hers. "I need to fuck you."

"Oh, God, yes!" Her hands were already on

his waistband, opening the button of his pants. "I was thinking of you all day."

He took that comment with a grain of salt. "What were you thinking about?"

"Your cock inside me."

Fuck! Talking like that made him even hotter. He captured her lips again, sealing them with a searing kiss.

He needed to take her now, before he lost it. His lips on hers, he reached into his pants pocket and pulled out a condom he'd shoved in there earlier. Then he pulled his pants and boxer briefs down to his knees, ripped the foil package open and slipped the condom onto his hard-on.

He put his hands on Olivia's shoulders, freed her of the bathrobe, and tossed it to the floor, before severing the kiss. Then he turned her to face the wall, eliciting a stunned gasp from her. But she didn't fight him, didn't protest. Instead, she braced herself with her palms against the wall, and spread her legs.

"Fuck!" he hissed and pushed her gown up over her hips, before he gripped them and pulled her back toward his groin. With a sharp exhale, he plunged into her pussy, seating himself to the hilt.

"Fuck, you're tight!" he growled, feeling utterly uncivilized.

Olivia moaned. "Then you'll just have to fuck me more often."

"I might just have to do that," he agreed and started pounding into her, thrusting deep and hard. He wanted to punish her for planning to kill him. Punish her for still playing the innocent woman who wanted him to take her, when she was clearly manipulating him into believing she posed no threat.

Jay rode her hard, and his mind went back to the night before, when she'd surrendered to him in bed, when she'd let herself go in his arms. Just like she surrendered now, taking his hard thrusts, and—judging by the moans that rolled over her lips—welcomed them.

"Oh, Jay, I wanna come," she begged. "Make me come."

He couldn't resist the siren's call and released her right hip. When he reached around her to her front, she took his hand and guided it to her pussy.

"There, right there," Olivia said, panting and pressing his fingers to her clit, before she placed her hand back on the wall to brace herself.

Jay stroked her clit in rhythm with his thrusts, and Olivia gasped. Her nightgown was sticking to her perspiring skin now, her breathing choppy, her pussy clenching around him on every withdrawal. All of a sudden, she shuddered, and her interior muscles spasmed, igniting his own orgasm. Semen shot through his cock and exploded from the tip, while waves of pleasure crashed over him, threatening to drown him. For a moment, his mind went blank, and all he could think of was how right it felt to be inside Olivia's sweet body. But then reality crashed over him, and he remembered why he was here: to figure out why she was planning to kill him. Fucking her against the wall hadn't been part of his plan. But maybe it would work in his favor after all, because what he needed tonight was for Olivia to be so exhausted that she would sleep like a log.

9

Olivia opened her eyes. She glanced at the clock on her bedside table. It was 2:17 a.m. and something had awoken her. She turned to snuggle closer to Jay, but she was alone.

Jay's visit had been a surprise, but a welcome one. And he'd been even more passionate than the night before. The way he'd touched and kissed her in the foyer had turned her on like nothing before. And when he'd taken her right there, pressed against the wall, she'd felt more wanted and desired than ever before in her life. She hadn't been able to move when he'd gripped her hips and pounded into her, but she'd loved every second of it. It had felt as if she belonged to him, to do with her as he pleased, and despite the fact that she prided herself on being an independent woman, she'd loved feeling him dominate her.

He'd dragged her to bed after they'd both climaxed in the foyer, and half an hour later, he'd made love to her again. This time face-to-face, but just as frantically as in the foyer. She'd fallen asleep shortly later. But now she was awake, and Jay wasn't in her bed anymore. Had he left?

Olivia swung her legs out of bed and grabbed her nightgown. She slipped it over her head and walked outside into the hallway. She saw immediately that there was light in her office, and the door was ajar. She pushed it open and froze.

Jay, wearing only boxer briefs, was rifling through her office. He was opening drawers and pulling out files.

"What the fuck are you doing?"

He spun around to face her, sucking in an audible breath. His facial expression told her that he knew he was caught doing something he shouldn't do.

"It's not what it looks like."

The cliché rolled off his lips so easily that she realized that this wasn't the first time he was doing something so despicable. He was a professional at this, hired by somebody to seduce her and then find what everybody in the sci-fi genre wanted to know.

"Who sent you? Who?" It had to be one of the two sci-fi authors she was outselling.

"Nobody sent me."

"Was it Rick Sanders or John Marston? Which one of those fucking bastards paid you to find my manuscript? Who?" She stepped into the room, furious, and not at all afraid of him, even though he was so much taller and stronger than her. But the adrenaline pumping through her veins now lent her strength.

"Your manuscript? I wasn't looking for—"

"Don't lie to me! You fucking bastard, you were playing me all along. You only slept with me so you could get a look at my next book and then leak spoilers! Fuck you, Jay!"

"I don't know anything about a book," he insisted.

"Oh please! You're caught!" she spat. "As if you don't know who I really am. How stupid you must think I am! Are you gonna leak that to the press too? That you fucked the great sci-fi novelist T.R. Harland so you could reveal spoilers from the next book?" She felt tears rim her eyes, but she pushed them down. She wouldn't give him the satisfaction of crying in front of him. "So you could tell the world which character will get the axe next? So you can turn my fans against me and spoil my next release? You fucking jerk!"

He stared at her, almost paralyzed, surprise flickering in his eyes. "You're a novelist?"

"Fuck you, Jay! Don't pretend! What are they paying you, huh?"

"Nobody is paying me anything. I didn't know that you're a writer," he claimed and made a step toward her. "Olivia, I'm sorry, I—"

"Why are you still denying what you're doing? At least be a man, and admit that you were looking for my manuscript! For fuck's sake, I caught you going through my files!"

"Olivia, please, let me explain—"

"There's nothing to explain! You used me! You had sex with me so you could find what you were looking for. And I fell for it! Oh my God! How stupid! You were probably laughing behind my back about what an easy lay I am!"

That hurt even more than knowing that one of her rival authors had paid Jay to find her manuscript. But what Jay had done was personal. He'd pretended to care about her. He'd played the considerate lover. How naïve she'd been! Of course a handsome guy like Jay had no interest in somebody like her. She wasn't a beauty, just a decent looking woman. She had no model figure, nothing that men raved about. She was just a normal woman.

"I slept with you because I'm attracted to you. For no other reason," he said, his voice sounding resigned. "You have to believe me."

"I don't have to do anything!" she yelled. "Now get the fuck out of my house before I call the police and have you arrested for trespassing! And tell whoever hired you that if any part of my manuscript leaks before publication, I will sue them for every cent they've ever earned in their entire lives!"

"I'm sorry, Olivia, I truly am. I wish I could explain this to you, but I—"

"Get your fucking clothes, and leave!"

Finally, Jay moved. Olivia watched him walk into the bedroom, where he'd undressed in a hurry only hours earlier. A few moments later, he came back out, fully dressed this time. He looked at her, and parted his lips, as if he wanted to say something else, but he didn't.

Perhaps he'd finally realized that no excuse in the world would rectify the fact that he'd betrayed her trust. And hurt her like no other man had hurt her before.

When he left the cottage, she flipped the deadbolt and sucked a breath of air into her lungs. With it, the first sob tore from her chest. More followed. Within seconds tears flowed down her cheeks and dripped to the floor. But the tears couldn't wash away her pain. Jay had used her. Betrayed her. Their lovemaking had meant nothing to him. He'd only slept with her so he could search her home. And she'd been so stupid not to see through him right away.

Olivia felt shame engulf her. She'd behaved like a common slut tonight, letting him fuck her in the foyer only seconds after he'd entered her home unexpectedly. This was even worse than a booty call. Jay hadn't even called her to announce that he was coming over. He'd simply shown up, confident that she wouldn't turn him away.

He'd been so smooth that she guessed that this wasn't the first time he did something like this: seduce a woman so he could execute whatever task he'd been hired for. And she'd walked right into his trap.

10

Jay entered Ace's mansion before 6 a.m., tired and pissed off at himself. With the Metro not running until 5 a.m. and not wanting to risk taking a taxi—or worse, an Uber—Jay had walked the Mount Vernon Trail all the way from Alexandria to D.C. before reaching a Metro stop a few minutes after the trains were in service again.

The house was still quiet, but instead of going to his room to sleep, he walked into the computer room. Only a couple of desk lights illuminated the large room. Jay sat down in front of a computer, booted it up, and started searching the web for everything he could find on T.R. Harland. In his gut, he knew that Olivia had spoken the truth when she'd told him that she was indeed a sci-fi author and not an editor. But he had to confirm her claims nevertheless.

The references he found were clear in one point: nobody really knew who T.R. Harland was, whether a man or a woman. He read through the various articles and posts on different social media sites, and discovered that rumors that a beloved character in the *Galaxy Outcast* series that T.R. Harland wrote, would be killed off in the next book, and that there had been previous attempts by jealous individuals, whether they were authors, readers, or publishers, to leak spoilers of the plot and the character who would get the axe.

Olivia hadn't discussed wanting to kill him, but a character in her next book.

Jay cursed. "Fuck!"

From the far corner of the room, he suddenly heard a noise, and he jumped up.

Fox rose from behind a computer

workstation. "Oh, I must've dozed off for a minute." He blinked. "What time is it?"

"Past six," Jay said.

"What happened?"

"Did you watch the surveillance cameras?" Jay asked, suddenly realizing something. The camera in the foyer had recorded him fucking Olivia. He quickly switched to the computer that streamed the surveillance footage and woke up the screen.

"Only until you showed up in her house. Figured you had it in hand. And you did."

"How much did you see?"

Fox rolled his eyes. "Don't worry, I stopped watching when I realized you were getting down to business." He rubbed his neck. "I was too busy with hacking into Olivia's cell phone records anyway. I was just waiting for them to download, when I must have closed my eyes for a moment." He looked at the screen. "Oh, looks like I got everything I need." He sat down behind the computer.

Jay sighed with relief. At least nobody had seen the video. He had to delete it, before anybody could see him fucking Olivia. She didn't deserve that kind of violation of her privacy.

"Looks like she called her sister," Fox said and stood up again. "So we might have two murdering sisters on our hands."

Jay swiveled with his chair. "No, we don't."

"Hey, Jay, I know you like the girl, but—"

"She's not a killer. She's an author, and she was discussing a scene about killing off one of the characters in her next book."

Fox furrowed his forehead and approached. "Did she tell you that?"

Jay let out a breath. "I pieced it together after she tossed me out on my ass."

"What?"

In as few words as possible, he filled Fox in on what had transpired between him and Olivia, though he glossed over the fact that he'd fucked her in the foyer. Then he showed him what he'd found on the author T.R. Harland.

"I know it's not definitive proof that she's the author, since there are no photos or anything else, but I know in my gut that she didn't lie to me."

"Fuck! That was bad luck," Fox said. "But I can dig a little deeper. There should be a paper trail. After all, the author has to get paid by the publisher. It shouldn't be too hard to find the payments and see where they lead us. And I already have Olivia's Social Security number. I'll pull up her tax returns and see what she's reporting. Why don't you get a little shut-eye or take a shower, while I take care of this?"

"You must be just as tired. Maybe I can help you. By the way, I thought you and Michelle don't stay here overnight."

Fox shrugged. "When one of our own is in danger, it's all-hands-on-deck. But looks like tonight Michelle and I get to sleep in our own bed again. Just as long as all this checks out."

"Good. Coffee?"

"I won't say no to that," Fox said.

"Oh, and don't let anybody look at the surveillance footage. I need to erase part of it." Just as soon as Fox had confirmed Olivia's identity.

Fox tossed him a curious look. "Do I wanna know what and why?"

"No, you don't."

Fox smirked. "You horndog!"

Jay flipped him the bird and left the computer room.

In the kitchen, Jay was surprised to see that Phoebe was already up. She wore a nightgown and a bathrobe over it. It was open in the front, her pregnancy belly too large for the bathrobe to fit her. For a moment, he just looked at her belly and envied Ace. He would have a family soon.

"Morning, Phoebe."

She turned her head and smiled at him. "Good morning, Tiger. You're back."

"Yeah." Jay walked to the coffee machine and started making coffee.

"Didn't go well, did it?"

"More like the opposite of well," he confirmed.

"Hmm." Phoebe seemed to understand that he didn't want to talk about it. She went to the refrigerator, took a bottle of water from it, and left the kitchen.

Jay took his time to make coffee. He poured two cups and went back to the computer room. Fox wasn't alone anymore. Michelle sat at the computer station next to his and was typing on the keyboard. When Michelle tossed him a regretful look, he knew that Fox had filled her in.

"Hey," Jay said and handed one cup to Michelle and the other to Fox.

"But that was meant for you," Michelle said.

"No, no, take it. I'll get myself another one," Jay said and went back to the kitchen again. When he returned with his cup of coffee, Fox motioned him to approach.

"Got something?"

"Yes," Fox replied. "I first checked Olivia Morikawa's tax returns. And her only income stems from a K-1."

"A K-1?"

"Yes, it's a form that a partner or member gets from an LLC. So I looked into the LLC. The only money the LLC makes comes from payments from one company, a publisher named Clarendon Press. One of their biggest authors is T.R. Harland. But I wanted to make absolutely sure that the payment was indeed for Harland. I was able to hack into their accounts. Honestly, they have really crappy online security in place. And I found the disbursements they made to Harland. They match the checks that the LLC received. So, yeah, Olivia told you the truth. She is T.R. Harland."

Jay sighed, relieved that she wasn't a psycho killer, but annoyed that he hadn't checked her out more thoroughly before he'd initiated contact with her. "Thanks, Fox, Michelle."

Michelle forced a smile. "And you can't really blame her for reacting the way she did when she saw you going through her stuff. There really are people out there who'd pay good money to leak her manuscript. From what I've read, some of the more established authors in her genre are annoyed that a newcomer is bumping them off the number one bestseller slots. She's pumped out six books in three years, while the others only publish one a year. I think there's a lot of jealousy going around. They want her to fail."

"I get it, I do. I just wish I'd known earlier. These are mistakes I can't come back from."

"What now?" Fox asked.

Jay shrugged and walked to the computer with the surveillance videos. "We have to keep watching the cottage. My premonitions are never wrong. Smith will show up there. In my premonition it was daytime, so let's concentrate on keeping an eye on the live feed during the day, and as long as we have the manpower, at night too. We have to be ready for it so we can figure out who he really is. Once the cameras in the house record his face, we can run it through facial recognition. Maybe we'll get a hit."

But first, Jay had to erase part of the recording. He found the spot where he entered the cottage the night before and had sex with Olivia in the foyer. Seeing himself and Olivia kiss and touch brought back every second of the previous night until the moment when she'd tossed him out of the house. His finger hovered over the delete button, but he hesitated. Erasing the recording of what he now knew was the last time he'd ever get to touch Olivia was harder than he'd thought. The tape kept replaying until the living room camera captured Olivia's face after Jay had left. Tears were streaming down her face, and the sobs made her chest heave.

Jay stretched his hand out toward the monitor wanting to console her. But he couldn't. He pressed the delete button, and wished that he could erase Olivia's pain just as easily.

11

The six bridesmaids Olivia's sister had chosen among her many friends were chatting excitedly as they admired Grace's beautiful gown. Olivia felt her heart constrict at her sister's beauty. Today, she would become Mrs. Timothy Bell, and everybody could see how happy Grace was. For Olivia, today's event was bittersweet. She was happy for her sister having found a man who worshipped the ground she walked on, but she would lose her best friend, plotting partner, and confidant, and they would never again be as close as they'd been since they were kids. And one other thing made today even sadder: Olivia didn't think that she'd ever find somebody who loved her as much as Timothy loved Grace, not after what had happened with Jay two days earlier.

She would have gone to the police had she not felt so ashamed for falling for Jay's lies, for making it so easy for him to execute his con. She hadn't even confided in her sister that she'd slept with Jay, and that he'd promptly betrayed her. She didn't want to spoil her sister's big day.

"I think you all need to go downstairs," Grace said now to the six girls. They were all dressed in different pastel colors, their sleeveless dresses reaching down to their ankles, and looked like fairies.

As the maid of honor, Olivia too was dressed in a long flowing silk dress which looked like she'd stepped out of a fairy tale.

When the girls closed the door of the hotel suite behind them, Grace turned to her, and reached for her hand. "I can't believe the day is finally here."

Olivia put on a brave smile. "I'm so happy

for you." She put her arms around her sister. "I can't wait to see you walk down that aisle. You've never been more beautiful, sis. Timothy is a lucky man."

Grace sniffled. "Now you're gonna make me cry and smudge my make-up."

They both chuckled.

"You'll see," Grace said, "one day you'll fall in love with a man like Timothy, and be just as happy."

She'd already met that man, but unfortunately their story didn't have a happy ending. "Yes, one day, I'm sure."

"I guess, I'm ready," Grace said with a look in the mirror.

"Almost," Olivia said, and walked to the table where she'd dropped a bag containing a box when she'd entered her sister's hotel room. She took the box out.

"Another present? But you already gave us—"

"This is really for Dad, since you couldn't have the wedding in Hawaii," Olivia said, and opened the box. Inside it lay a fresh Hawaiian lei made of fragrant pink plumerias.

"Oh Olivia! It's beautiful."

Olivia draped it around her sister's neck, careful not to disturb her hair, or to obstruct the pearl necklace she wore. Their eyes met in the mirror.

"It's perfect," Grace said.

There was a knock at the door.

"That'll be Dad," Olivia guessed and walked to the door.

She opened it. Her father, dressed in a dark suit, an orchid in his suit's buttonhole, stood there with a smile. He was suntanned. Since her parents had returned to live on Oahu, her father was surfing again in his native Hawaii, and he'd never looked happier.

Her parents had arrived in D.C. on the red-eye the morning after she'd thrown Jay out of her cottage. They were staying in the same hotel where the wedding was taking place. In fact, Olivia had taken a room here too, so she didn't have to go back home to Alexandria late at night.

"Your mother is already downstairs. They're all waiting."

Olivia ushered her father into the room, and

let the door fall shut behind him. When Grace turned around to greet her father, he stood still for a moment, his eyes drinking her in.

"My little girl has grown up to be a woman." Tears welled up in his eyes. "It's like only yesterday that you were playing in the sand." He reached for Grace's hands and clasped them. "You're wearing a lei."

"It was Olivia's idea."

Her father turned to her and smiled, a tear loosening from his eye. She put her arms around him, and kissed him on the cheek.

"I love you both so much," he said. "You're so grown up, my girls. And more beautiful with each day."

"You're making me cry, Dad," Grace said.

He chuckled, and it wasn't difficult to see why their mother had fallen in love with the handsome surfer. There was warmth in his laugh, and kindness, and a pinch of mischief.

"I leave the crying to your mother. There'll be plenty of that today," he claimed. "Now, shall we go down there and wow them all?"

He offered both arms, one to each of his daughters, and together they left the hotel room and walked down the long hallway to the elevators.

Olivia wondered whether one day it would be her turn to be the one in the white dress, being led down the aisle by her father, to a handsome man who loved her.

"And just so you two know, I want at least two dances with each of you, no matter how many handsome young men are vying for your attention," he said with a grin. Then he winked and looked at Olivia. "And I've seen some of Timothy's friends. I think you'll have your pick of handsome young men today, Olivia."

She rolled her eyes. "Are you trying to play matchmaker, Dad?"

"It worked with your sister."

"And it was embarrassing," Grace claimed, laughing. "You can't just walk up to a stranger in a restaurant and ask him if he wants to go out on a date with your daughter."

"Timothy didn't mind," he said, chuckling, "or we wouldn't be celebrating a wedding today. Besides, he wasn't a complete stranger. He lived in the same building as your mom and I. We practically knew each other. And I never heard any weird sounds coming from his condo."

"We're never gonna win this argument, sis," Olivia said. "Better not waste our breath."

Grace winked. "Yeah, we need that for dancing."

Olivia smiled. Her father had a way about him that always cheered her up.

12

Jay walked into the computer room, freshly showered and dressed, a bagel in his hand. It was two in the afternoon. He'd gone to bed at five in the morning, at which time Yankee had taken over watching the surveillance cameras in Olivia's cottage. During the night nothing had happened. Olivia had gone to bed early, and nobody had entered or left the cottage.

Yankee was sitting in front of the computer, staring into the monitor, his feet up on the desk. He turned his head when Jay entered.

"Hey," Yankee said. "Got some sleep in?"

"Yeah." Jay pointed to the monitor. "Anything happen?"

"Not much. Olivia got up around eight and got ready pretty quickly. Didn't even have breakfast. She packed a bag and left the house."

Surprised, Jay stepped closer. "She packed a bag? Can you replay the tape?"

"Sure thing." Yankee took his feet off the desk and rolled his chair closer, so he could type on the keyboard. "Here you go."

Jay watched as Olivia, dressed in jeans and a casual T-shirt, went in and out of her bedroom, though he couldn't see what she was doing in the bedroom, since he hadn't placed a camera there. After a few minutes, she emerged with a small black travel bag and placed it next to the sofa in the living room. Then she walked back into the hallway and appeared on the camera in the office. She opened the closet, and took out a long dress. It was wrapped in a plastic sleeve like the ones similar to what dry cleaners used. The dress was a soft pastel of greens and blues. She closed the closet door, then walked back into the living room, looked around as if trying to make sure that she hadn't forgotten anything, before she grabbed the travel bag and dress and left the cottage.

"What day is today?" Jay asked.

"Saturday, why?"

"That's it. She's going to her sister's wedding." A wedding she'd invited him to attend as her date. Before she'd thrown him out of her house.

Behind Jay, the door opened. He looked over his shoulder and saw Lilly enter with a tray of food.

"Hey, Jack, I brought you some food," she said with a smile.

Yankee rose and walked up to her, kissed her on the lips, and took the tray from her. "Thanks, baby, I'm starving."

"I can take over here," Jay said. "Take a break."

"You sure?"

Jay nodded. "Where's everybody else?"

"Scott is outside with Phoebe. She's not feeling well, so they're walking a little in the backyard. Maybe the fresh air will help her."

"Sorry to hear that," Jay said. "Will she be all right?"

Lilly nodded confidently. "Don't worry about her. The pregnancy isn't easy on her. I think it's all the stress that's getting to her. I did an ultrasound on her this morning, and the baby looks fine."

"You took her to the doctor?"

"No, I managed to get a portable ultrasound machine delivered." She winked. "Michelle is really good at procuring anything we need. At least that way I can be useful."

Yankee chuckled. "You're always useful."

Lilly blushed, and Jay had to look away. It was hard to be in the presence of happy couples like Yankee and Lilly and the others, when he knew that he'd blown it with Olivia.

"Where are Fox and Michelle?" Jay asked to change the subject.

"They're setting up surveillance outside of Langley," Lilly replied.

"What? Are they crazy? They shouldn't go anywhere near the CIA."

"Can't be avoided," Yankee said. "They need to capture the license plates of every car entering and exiting the CIA's parking lot to help us determine whether Smith works for the CIA."

Jay shook his head. "That's risky."

Yankee shrugged. "Risky was Fox breaking into Langley to get behind their firewall. At least this time, he's staying outside. They're installing the cameras on all the roads leading into Langley. And once we get the feeds from those cameras, we can cross-reference the cars with data from the DMV."

"Not everybody at the CIA will have a license plate that can be traced. Some of them will have blocked plates."

"Yeah, but mostly the covert agents. Smith strikes me more as a guy who's in management. So with some luck, his license plate won't be blocked."

"I hope they know what they're doing," Jay said.

"We can't just sit around and wait until Smith shows up in Olivia's house. You know as well as I do that you can't know *when* your premonition will come true."

He knew that, which made everything even

more frustrating. Having to watch Olivia's cottage day-in and day-out to wait for Smith to show up was like pouring salt into an open wound. Every time he looked at the feed from the cottage, he was reminded of what had passed between him and Olivia, and what an idiot he'd been, letting her catch him while searching her office.

"I know," Jay admitted. "Go, take a break. I'll hold down the fort."

"We'll be out on the terrace if you need us," Yankee said. "Just use the intercom if you need me to come back in."

"No problem."

Yankee and Lilly left and closed the door behind them. Silence fell over the room. Jay directed his eyes back to the computer monitor where the screen was split into four squares, each of them showing a different room in the cottage. In a way he was grateful that Olivia was at the wedding and not at home. When he'd watched the monitor during the night, he'd felt like a dirty voyeur, and guilty even though he knew he couldn't remove the cameras before Smith showed his face and they could track him to wherever he lived. Until then, he would have to continue watching Olivia's house, and by extension, Olivia herself as she went about her life. Until then, there was no use in even trying to forget Olivia. Being reminded of her on a daily basis made that as impossible as forgetting to breathe.

For a moment, he wondered what it would have been like to accompany Olivia to her sister's wedding, holding her hand while they watched the happy couple say their vows, dancing with Olivia, and holding her in his arms. But that was just a pipe dream, something that would never come true, no matter how much he wished for it.

Jay took a deep breath, trying to clear his mind, when he suddenly saw bouquets of flowers appear in front of him. He blinked, but the pink and white flowers were still there. They now mixed with green leaves and pink bows, white candles, and silver ribbons. As the picture zoomed out, he realized he was looking at a decorated table. White linen covered the round table, and on the chairs that surrounded it, well-dressed women and men chatted and laughed, and drank from their champagne glasses. More tables with more well-dressed guests appeared, and Jay realized that this was a wedding reception. He let his eyes roam to see if he recognized anybody and if he could figure out where this event was taking place.

Dance music suddenly drifted to his ears, and people started to rise from their seats. At first, Jay couldn't see where they were heading, but then, for a moment he had a clear view of a bridal gown, though he couldn't see the bride's face. Around her neck hung a lei. Was this wedding taking place in Hawaii? He looked at the other guests, but it appeared that the bride was the only one wearing a lei.

A man in his late fifties, early sixties took the bride's hand, and Jay caught a glimpse of his face. He was definitely Asian, most likely Japanese. Yet most of the guests were white. When the Japanese man turned the bride toward him, Jay could finally see her face. She was Japanese too. Was this man the father of the bride? Very likely. Jay looked more closely at the bride. He'd seen her before. Not too long ago in fact, though not in person. He'd seen a photo of her: in Olivia's cottage.

This was Grace, Olivia's sister. And this was her wedding. Grace began dancing with her father, the eyes of all the guests on them, while a young man in a tuxedo danced with an older white woman, which Jay assumed was the groom's mother. As they twirled to the music, Jay suddenly perceived a different movement at the right lower edge of the scene playing out in front of his mental eye. His trained eye recognized the gun immediately. But he could only see the sleeve of the man holding it. He fired into the crowd, sending the guests scrambling for cover, paving a clear path to the two dancing couples.

The next bullet hit the bride in the chest, and blood seeped through the virginal white bustier. Her father, still holding his daughter in his arms, trying to shield her, was struck by the next bullet. It hit him in the neck, and both father and daughter tumbled to the ground. More shots were fired amidst the screams of the guests, and just then, he saw Olivia, dressed in the blue-green-pastel dress he'd seen on the surveillance tape, running onto the dance floor.

The scream that burst from Olivia's lips tore his heart into a thousand pieces. She crouched down to her father and her sister, and pressed her bare hands onto their bleeding wounds trying to stem the blood loss, but there was no movement, no breath left in either of them. They were both gone.

She turned her head suddenly, and Jay saw that the groom held the older woman he'd danced with in his arms. She was shot in the back, and the groom had been hit in the shoulder.

"Mom!" Olivia screamed and ran toward the older woman, tears streaming down her face. "No, Mom, no!!!"

Jay's heart clenched in pain. He'd been wrong when he'd assumed that the groom had been dancing with his own mother. He'd been dancing with the bride's mother. As he dropped to his knees to lower her onto the ground, Jay saw the older woman's face and recognized that there was no life left in her eyes.

In the space of ten seconds, Olivia was left with nothing. Everybody she loved was gone.

As the premonition blurred, Jay knew that no matter the cost to himself, he had to prevent this tragedy. If he didn't, he would never be able to live with this guilt. He owed her.

13

The wedding ceremony had been beautiful, and Olivia, as well as her mother, had shed a few tears of joy. Even though Olivia had helped her sister with the guest list and handled the RSVPs, she was overwhelmed by the number of guests, and the fact that she barely recognized any faces among them. She knew all six bridesmaids, and a couple of her sister's male friends and colleagues, but everybody else was from the groom's side.

The ceremony had taken place mid-afternoon, and after drinks and light hors d'oeuvres, during which the happy couple disappeared with the photographer, Olivia had snuck back into her hotel room. The exclusive five-star hotel was brand-new and located in Northeast Washington D.C. with extensive gardens and world-class amenities, including multiple pools, a spa, and several ballrooms perfect for weddings and other large events.

Thanks to the groom's connections to the son of the hotel manager, Olivia and the other guests who wanted to stay the night, had received discounted rates. Olivia's room was almost as big as her entire cottage, and she'd never stayed anywhere more luxurious. But that wasn't the reason she snuck back into her room, where she'd changed into her dress earlier in the day. No, she just couldn't keep smiling for so long, when inside she wanted to cry.

She knew it was stupid to still be upset about Jay's betrayal. He certainly didn't deserve her tears. Still, she was disappointed in herself. She'd always thought of herself as a good judge of character, but apparently that was only the case when it concerned fictional characters. When it came to real people, she was lousy at recognizing jerks.

But taking refuge in her hotel room was only temporary. When her mother texted her that dinner was about to be served, she had to return to the reception and play the happy sister and maid of honor. Neither her father nor her mother knew what she was going through, and she had no intention of telling them about it. They were here for only a few days, and she didn't want to sour the happy occasion by burdening them with her problems.

So she put on a brave face again and rejoined the wedding party. The seating order had been meticulously planned, and Olivia remembered that she, Grace, and Timothy had sat together many evenings to figure out what would be best to avoid any strife between certain guests. Since Timothy's parents were divorced, and certain factions of his family were not speaking to other parts of his family, this wasn't an easy task. Olivia swore to herself that if she ever got married, it would be an intimate affair.

Olivia ended up sitting with two other bridesmaids, and Ella, a distant female cousin of Timothy, as well as four college buddies of the groom. One of the bridesmaids had already had way too many glasses of champagne in the afternoon and was so tipsy that she laughed at everything anybody at the table said. When two of Timothy's college friends exchanged conspiratorial looks, Olivia could already guess what they were thinking. One of them, or both, would try to get the girl into bed before the night was over.

Normally, Olivia would have kept an eye on her fellow bridesmaid so that this wouldn't happen. But she'd overheard the girl earlier, telling one of the other bridesmaids that tonight she would get her hands on a hunky young man and get laid. But since she was shy, she needed a few drinks to accomplish the task. And who was Olivia to stand in the way of the age-old tradition of bridesmaids having sex with groomsmen?

Maybe she should do the same, sleep with one of the handsome guys present. And there were plenty to choose from. At her own table, one of them started flirting with her. But for some reason she just couldn't get into the mood to flirt back, no matter how hard she tried. She gave up on it, and instead struck up a conversation with Timothy's cousin Ella from Wisconsin. She appeared shy, and none of the guys seemed to take any notice of her.

Olivia was glad, when the dessert course finally arrived. It meant it was time for the speeches, and she didn't have to make conversation for a while. Like everybody else, she turned to look at Timothy, who talked first, recounting how he and Grace had met, and how they'd fallen in love. Speeches by the best man, then by her father, and finally by Grace herself followed, though Olivia barely listened.

When she heard clapping, she joined in, before turning back to her dessert. She hadn't touched it. She wasn't hungry. It was a wonder that she'd managed to eat some of the main course.

"Are you not having your dessert?" Ella asked.

"No, do you want it?"

"If you're not eating it. It's delicious," Ella said.

Olivia handed it to her, glad that it didn't go to waste. "Enjoy. I'm already so full today."

The waiters started to clear the tables, and Olivia folded her napkin and placed it on the table. "Excuse me. I'll go freshen up a little."

She made her way past the tables, dodging guests who also took this opportunity to stretch their legs, go outside to smoke, or head for the restroom. Or those who wanted to simply escape the next part of the reception: the dancing. Had she merely been a guest, not the maid of honor and the bride's sister, she would have left the wedding reception at this point, and nobody would even have noticed it. But she couldn't do that. Her parents would notice, and so would Grace. And then Grace would wonder if anything was wrong with her. And no bride should have to worry about anything on her wedding day.

There was a line outside the ladies' room, so Olivia decided to use the one in the other wing of the hotel. It would be quieter there. She was right. She was the only person in the elegant ladies' room. It smelled of expensive soap, and soft music played inside, making her feel like she was in a spa. At least, she could take a few breaths here and collect her strength before she had to rejoin the wedding party to play her part as best she could.

To think that she'd asked Jay to attend as her date seemed so unreal now. What had she been thinking? Just because the sex was so good? And by God, the sex had been amazing. Never before had a man made her feel like that. She shook off the thoughts. There was no use crying over spilled milk. There would be other men. Honest men. She hoped.

Determined not to waste another thought on Jay, she left the ladies' room. She walked only a few steps, when she passed by an alcove with a telephone. The alcove wasn't empty. Inside, the tipsy bridesmaid from her table was kissing one of Timothy's friends, and by the sounds they made, it was clear that they would soon find a more private place, or they would risk being thrown out of the hotel.

Olivia almost wanted to chuckle. If a tipsy bridesmaid could land a hunky guy just by batting her eyelashes at him and laughing at everything the guy said, then why couldn't she do that? After all, she was the bride's sister, the maid of honor, and she wasn't bad looking. There had to be at least one guy among the guests, whose bucket list contained fucking a bridesmaid. How hard could it be?

Is that what you really want? Screw just any guy?

She hated it when her conscience got in the way of her having fun. Why was she so uptight? Couldn't she let loose for once and just go with the flow, and do something reckless?

"Oh!" The gasp came from the tipsy bridesmaid.

Only now, Olivia realized that she was still standing there, staring into the alcove. They both stared at her as if she was a voyeur taking pleasure in watching other people be intimate. She felt herself blush.

"Oh, sorry," she said quickly, searching for an excuse. "Damn sandals." She crouched down and pretended to adjust the straps.

"Let's... uh..." the guy said, and took the bridesmaid's hand to lead her away.

When Olivia stood up again, she saw them head for the elevators. Well, at least somebody was getting what they wanted. Maybe one day, she would be as bold as the tipsy bridesmaid and just do what she wanted and not give a damn about what anybody thought.

14

Jay gripped the steering wheel tighter. "How much longer?"

Next to him, Yankee looked at the navigation on his phone. "Four minutes. Take a left here."

They were the only ones in the white van they'd hastily disguised as a laundry service. After Jay's terrifying premonition, he'd alerted everybody at the mansion. Ace had quickly figured out where and when Grace Morikawa's wedding was taking place, while Lilly had helped Yankee and Jay dress up like waiters and disguise their faces with beards and glasses. Going to a large event in a big hotel meant that the chances of being recognized by somebody were astronomical. But it couldn't be helped.

By the time Ace got the address, Jay and Yankee were ready to leave. Ace couldn't come with them. He had to take over monitoring Olivia's cottage in case Smith showed up there while she was gone. And Lilly was looking after Phoebe, who still suffered from morning sickness, even though it was early evening. Fox and Michelle hadn't yet returned from their mission.

"We'll make it," Yankee assured him now. "It's early yet. If it's like any other wedding, they've probably not even finished dinner yet. And the dancing is always after dinner."

Jay hoped Yankee was right. In the distance he saw the hotel. "There it is."

"Drive around the side. From what I could see from the pictures on their website, the ballrooms overlook the gardens in the back. There's a service entrance on the left where they unload deliveries. We shouldn't have a problem getting in there."

"Yeah. Good idea. It was smart of you to check the pictures on their websites to see what their service staff wears. With a bit of luck, we'll blend right in."

Their black pants and white shirts with black bow ties were close enough to the photos of the waitstaff at the hotel. And the hotel was large and new enough for two strange faces not to attract too much attention.

Jay parked the white van between a larger catering truck and a hedge, hiding the vehicle from curious eyes. He left the key in the ignition in case they had to make a quick getaway and jumped out of the van.

Casting furtive looks around them, Jay and Yankee hurried toward the door and entered the building. This was an area the hotel guests never saw. The corridor led to different storage and service areas, such as staging areas for arriving groceries and other supplies. Racks with table linen and cleaning supplies lined the hallway. There were cardboard boxes with flower arrangements and other trinkets. From the end of the hallway, Jay noticed an employee come toward them. He wore black pants and a white shirt, but he also wore a tuxedo jacket.

"Hey you two," the man called out to Jay and Yankee. "Where are your fucking jackets? It's formal dress today. This is not a Motel Six."

"Of course, sorry, a guest puked all over us," Jay lied. "We were just looking for new ones."

The waiter pointed past them. "You just passed the laundry, you idiots."

Jay and Yankee had no choice but to turn on their heels.

"First door on the left," the man instructed and added under his breath, "New people."

Jay entered the room and saw several tuxedo jackets hanging on a rail. He grabbed one, slipped it on, and Yankee did the same, before they rushed outside again, continuing toward the interior of the hotel. The other waiter had disappeared.

Jay pushed the door open, and found himself in the public part of the hotel. Rich red and gold colors dominated the elegant foyer.

Yankee, who'd studied the floorplan of the hotel, instructed, "To the right."

"I hear music," Jay said. He sped up, but there were guests around, and other hotel personnel as they passed the reception area, and he couldn't run, or he would only draw attention upon himself.

"Almost there," Yankee whispered.

"Sir, sir," an older lady coming from a hallway to Jay's left, said.

Jay didn't stop, but the woman was persistent.

"I can't find the elevators," she said, a helpless look on her face.

"I'll take care of it," Yankee said and turned to the woman. "Ma'am, just turn to your right, past the reception, and there you'll find the elevators."

Jay pulled his earpiece from his pants pocket and inserted it in his ear. By the time Yankee caught up with him, Jay already saw a sign outside the palm-flanked entrance to a ballroom. *Welcome to the Bell-Morikawa Wedding Reception*, it said. *Private Event, Invited Guests Only.*

His heart was hammering in his chest. Dance music came from inside the ballroom. By his calculations, they had only a minute or two until the shooter would kill Olivia's family.

"I'll go right, you go left," Jay ordered, and they entered the large ballroom. Around the perimeter, small palm trees, decorated with pink flowers and white tulle bows stood in terracotta pots, making the venue look like it was outdoors. From the ceiling, palm branches hung suspended, building a canopy. In between, sparkling lights gave the impression of stars in the night sky.

The guests were gathering in a circle around the dance floor, only a woman in a wheelchair was sitting, and a young man now rolled her toward the dance floor. In the far corner, a band was playing, and in another corner, bamboo partitions provided an area for the waitstaff to deal with dishes, open bottles of wine and champagne, and refill water pitchers. A waiter was busy carrying a full tray of dirty dishes out through a door at that end.

"Do you see him?'" Jay asked, speaking quietly into his microphone, while he searched the crowd and the areas behind the palm trees for the shooter.

"Nothing so far," came Yankee's reply.

Where the fuck was the shooter hiding? He looked at the crowd. Everybody was looking toward the two couples that now started to dance. Nobody took any notice of Jay or Yankee. Even the two waiters who'd been bussing tables, had stopped their work and were watching the dancing couples.

"Fuck," Yankee suddenly hissed through the earpiece.

"Where is he?" Jay shot Yankee a look. He was near the area where the band was playing.

"Smith. Smith is here."

Jay's heart skipped a beat. "Fuck!"

He followed Yankee's gaze and saw him too. He was dressed as elegantly as the rest of the guests, his eyes directed toward the dancing couples. From his vantage point, Jay couldn't see if he was carrying a weapon, but it was possible.

"Keep an eye on him. Don't let him see you," Jay said, when he suddenly perceived a movement to his right. From behind the bamboo partition, a man suddenly emerged. He wasn't a waiter, but dressed in a suit and tie. A guest, but clearly not one who'd been invited.

"The shooter," Jay alerted Yankee. "Behind the bamboo partition."

Jay sprinted toward the man who looked to be in his mid-thirties, when he saw him reach underneath his jacket, trying to pull something from it. Jay barreled toward him just as he cleared the partition, and the shooter produced a handgun. Jay crashed into him with such force that the guy lost his balance and fell back against the partition. As he tumbled backward, Jay snatched his hand holding the gun and wrestled it from him, before he put him in a chokehold.

"Fucking bastard," he hissed.

15

Olivia took a deep breath and headed back into the reception, when she froze at the entrance. All the guests were gathered around the dance floor, watching two couples dance. Her father was dancing with Grace, and her mother with Timothy. The music was loud, and everybody was focused on the dancers, which was why nobody noticed what Olivia saw.

A tall, black waiter lunged for a man who emerged from behind a partition where several shelving units held bottles of wine, and plastic baskets with dirty dishes. The man wasn't a waiter. He would have looked like a guest, were it not for the weapon in his hand. Olivia's heart stopped. The black waiter tackled the armed man and wrestled the gun from him. Just then, another waiter, a tall blond guy, appeared from another direction and snatched the weapon from the floor, then stuck it in the back of his pants, while the first waiter put the would-be shooter into a chokehold.

She'd seen enough cop shows to know that the person administering the chokehold had to be professional law enforcement. When he loosened his hold on the attacker's neck, the man slumped forward, unconscious.

When the two heroic waiters suddenly looked in her direction, she realized that she'd walked halfway toward them, and was now only a few feet away from them. Close enough to see the black waiter's face more clearly. He sported a goatee, and his black hair was curly and thick. He wore horn-rimmed glasses, but there was nothing wrong with his eyes. She recognized those eyes. This wasn't some random waiter, this was Jay, the man she'd slept with, the man who'd rifled through her office.

"Fuck," Jay hissed, his voice further confirming that it was him.

He exchanged a quick look with the other waiter, who she guessed wasn't a real waiter either. Both men were wearing secret-service-style earpieces in their ears.

"We've gotta get him outta here," the blond guy urged.

Jay nodded, and each of them took one arm of the unconscious man and looped it over his shoulder. Then Jay cast her a look. "Olivia, you didn't see me. This never happened. Please."

Then he and his partner disappeared through the door behind the bamboo partition, dragging the subdued man with them. How could she pretend that this hadn't happened? No, she couldn't just forget that. Jay was a hero, yet he wanted her to pretend she hadn't seen him take down a shooter? So much didn't make sense. How could the same man betray her trust by rifling through her private things, yet risk his own life to take down a shooter at her sister's wedding?

She cast a quick glance over her shoulder, where the two couples were still dancing, and the guests were still watching them. Nobody had noticed what had happened.

Determined to talk to Jay, she followed him through the door into the service area of the hotel. Jay and his partner were already halfway down the corridor.

"Jay, hold up!" she called after him.

He cast a quick glance over his shoulder. "Go back to the wedding, Olivia."

Suddenly another waiter emerged from a door and looked at the two men dragging the unconscious one. "What's going on here?"

"Guy can't hold his liquor," Jay replied.

"Yeah, there's always one, isn't there?" Jay's partner added. "We'll just put him in a taxi."

"Yeah, get him outta here," the waiter said, then glanced in Olivia's direction. "Is he with you?"

"Yeah, uh," Olivia said and approached

hurriedly, "my brother-in-law. He's an alcoholic. Sorry, he should have never been invited to the wedding." The lie rolled off her lips like well-rehearsed dialogue from one of her books. Sometimes it paid to be a professional writer.

Olivia exchanged a look with Jay, and finally he nodded. "Let's get him a taxi, ma'am. Come with us so you can give the taxi driver his address."

She followed them through the corridor, around a couple of turns, until they finally reached a door that led outside. There, Jay and his partner headed toward a white van. She remained on their heels and watched them open the side door of the van. *Brilliant White Laundry Service* it said. With every moment that passed, she became more suspicious of the entire incident.

"What is this?" she asked, and Jay stepped aside, all of a sudden giving her a close view of the face of the unconscious man. She froze. "Oh my God." She pointed at the man. "That can't be."

"What?" Jay asked and stared from her to the man he'd subdued. "Do you know him?"

Olivia nodded. "That's Dirk Clover. He worked in the same architecture firm as my sister." Her heart beat out of control. "He started stalking her, and it got so bad that the firm fired him, and Grace got a restraining order against him." She looked away from Dirk's face to Jay and his partner. "Is that why you're here? Somebody informed you that he violated the restraining order? Oh my God, he really tried to kill her, didn't he?"

That knowledge sent an ice-cold shiver down her spine despite the warm evening weather.

"Are you law enforcement? Is that why you're here?" She pointed to Jay's face. "Disguised with a fake beard and hair?

"We're not police."

"Then what are you? Those earpieces don't look cheap. And that chokehold you used on him looked professional."

She noticed Jay and his partner exchange a look.

"I'll take care of him," the blond guy said. "You'd better sort this out with her. We can't let this get out."

Something in his words made her suspicious. "What does he mean by take care of him?" She looked the blond guy up and down, and noticed that his beard didn't look all that natural either. "We have to call the police to get him arrested. He tried to kill my sister." And perhaps Timothy too.

"We can't do that," the blond guy said.

"But I saw it all. I can testify. He'll go down for attempted murder."

"We can't go to the police," Jay said. "Nobody can know that we were here today—"

"But you're heroes. You saved my sister, and who knows how many others he would have shot."

"Olivia, you must believe me when I tell you that we can't go to the police. Yan—my friend and I can't go to the authorities. We have to do this our way."

She gasped. "You're wanted by the police."

Jay shrugged. "Not by the police, no. But if the police have us on their radar, soon our enemies will too." He addressed his partner, "Make sure this scumbag knows we'll kill him if he ever comes anywhere near Grace's family again."

"Not a problem. I'll make sure to pound it into him, so he won't forget it anytime soon." The blond guy slid the side door of the van closed. "Be careful."

Jay nodded, then turned fully to her, while his eyes roamed their surroundings as if checking to see if anybody was watching them. "I wish you hadn't recognized me. I had no intention of spoiling this day for you. But since you saw what happened, I owe you an explanation. But we can't be anywhere in public. Nobody must overhear us."

Olivia nodded. "I have a room in the hotel. We can go there to talk." She turned toward the service entrance, but Jay stopped her.

"We'll go in the other entrance." Then he shrugged out of the tuxedo jacket he wore and tossed it behind a bush, loosened his bow tie and rid himself of it too. "It's best if we look like a couple. We'll blend in more easily. You mind?"

He reached for her hand, and she took it. It reminded her of the evening when he'd walked her home from the restaurant. Was it stupid of her to allow this? To invite him to her hotel room where they would be alone, and where nobody would come to her aid if she needed it? At the same time, she recalled the moment when she'd noticed the gun in Dirk's hand. There was no doubt in her mind that Grace's stalker had planned to kill the bride and groom. And Jay and his partner had prevented the tragedy. She owed him her gratitude for this heroic action. If he really meant her any harm, he could have tossed her in the van with Dirk, and driven off with his partner, without anybody noticing.

When they reached the elevators, Olivia looked up at him. Who was Jay really? A thief for hire? A reluctant hero? Or something else altogether? Because for sure he wasn't some meek yoga instructor. The way he'd acted only minutes earlier was evidence that his training was rooted in something else. Military, if she had to guess, since he denied being in law enforcement. Still, nothing that she'd seen today explained why he had searched her cottage. That act didn't fit at all with what had happened today. But she wouldn't stop asking questions until she had all the answers she needed to determine if Jay was worth caring about. Because she still cared about him, despite him betraying her trust.

16

Smith emerged from behind a large planter in the foyer of the hotel, which he'd used to hide behind so the man he'd spotted walking toward the elevator in the company of the bride's sister, didn't spot him. He'd stepped out of the ballroom to make a phone call after the bride and groom had danced with the bride's parents, and then invited other guests to join them on the dance floor. Smith wasn't interested in dancing. Dancing was something for happy people. And he wasn't happy.

Jones was breathing down his neck about the slow progress of their plan. Even though

Smith was doing everything to get the new facility up and running after the ex-Stargate agents had blown up the old facility, progress crept along at a snail's pace. It hadn't helped that one of their key scientists had been killed during the attack, together with several of the supporting personnel, though those were easily replaceable. The head scientist was not. And Smith's own expertise didn't extend into neurological science.

At least, he'd been able to save the brain scans they'd already undertaken, and Smith had fed the data into the prototype that would soon be a fully functioning quantum computer. However, the computer would only be as good as the data it received, which meant more data was needed. More former Stargate agents were needed. He had to extract that data from their brains that was responsible for their precognitive skills, that part of their brain that gave them their gift of foresight.

Once sufficient quantities of good data were fed into the computer, artificial intelligence would take over and create a machine that would be able to precisely predict future world events. And whoever held the power of knowing the future in his hands would indeed be omnipotent, and rule not just the United States, but the world.

For now, he had to keep Jones happy, because without Jones's money and influence, the project would be dead on arrival. He would deal with Jones later. The only obstacle between him and that power were the members of the top-secret Stargate program. Their very gift was both a blessing and a curse. A blessing, because it enabled Smith to harness their powers, and a curse, because at any time they could have premonitions that would reveal all of Smith's plans. They knew too much already. Tiger, the agent they'd rescued before Smith's people had been able to complete the brain scan, had witnessed too much. Some of his secrets were out, and he could only hope that he'd remain a step ahead of them.

Smith glanced at the closing elevator doors. The tall black man with the goatee, the full hair, and the glasses, holding the hand of the bride's sister, had something familiar about him. It took only a couple of seconds, before he realized why. This was Jay Garner, ex-CIA Stargate agent, Code Name Tiger, the man who over two weeks ago had lain on a gurney about to have his brain scanned, when several ex-Stargate agents had rushed in, killed everybody, and saved Tiger. And here he was, holding hands with Olivia Morikawa, the maid of honor. What were the odds?

By the looks of it, Tiger was in a relationship with Olivia, or why else would they be holding hands and sneaking away from the wedding reception, no doubt heading to a room? He hadn't seen Tiger at the ceremony, nor the cocktail reception in the garden, or the dinner earlier. It appeared he wasn't an invited guest, otherwise he would have been there earlier and sat next to his date.

It wasn't hard to guess why he hadn't joined the party: he couldn't risk attending such a large event, particularly not in a place like Washington D.C. where he could be recognized by anybody connected to the CIA. He had to sneak around to see his girlfriend. And while his disguise was good, and most people wouldn't have realized who was hiding beneath the fake beard, hair, and glasses, Smith was familiar with all kinds of disguises and trained in spotting a fake beard from a distance.

He almost chuckled to himself. Tiger would lead him to the other agents, who were clearly harboring him somewhere. And then he'd get them all. It would be child's play. Soon, they would all be strapped to a gurney, and this time, Smith would drain every last brainwave from them. And to punish those bastards for messing with his plans, he'd make them watch when he killed the women helping them. Payback was a bitch.

"There you are."

He turned to the female voice behind him, and saw Evelyn approach. She looked stunning in her long silver dress, despite her age. At fifty-nine she was still beautiful and slim, but he was getting tired of her. Sleeping with her was boring, though luckily, she didn't initiate sex very often, and he had too many more important things on his mind to care. For now, she provided him with what he sought most:

connections and respectability. Soon, he wouldn't need any of it anymore, and then he would trade her in for somebody more suitable for a man with power.

He pasted a smile on his face. "Yes, dear?"

"I was looking for you. You promised to dance with me. What were you doing?"

"Apologies, I just had to take a call from the office."

"Everything all right?"

"Nothing to worry about." He took her hand. "Now, how about that dance?"

17

Jay followed Olivia into the hotel room and closed the door behind him. He removed his earpiece and shoved it in his pants pocket. Olivia had never looked lovelier, and for a moment, he drank in the sight, regretting that it was over between them. Still, he owed her an explanation so that she wouldn't disclose to anybody what she'd witnessed him and Yankee doing.

There was a moment of silence between them, and they simply stood a few feet apart, facing each other. He wasn't sure how to start. He wasn't prepared for this, because he hadn't expected Olivia to recognize him, but there was no use lamenting it now. Olivia wanted answers.

"How did you know what Dirk was planning?" she asked, her voice calm and collected now, though her breath had still not settled back into its normal rhythm, her chest rising under the silk fabric of her bridesmaid's dress.

She looked like a nymph or a mermaid, beautiful, petite, and vulnerable.

"I saw it."

She shook her head. "You saw him when you entered the ballroom? But why are you here in the first place? And disguised as a waiter. I don't get it."

"What I meant is that I had a premonition of what was about to happen here."

Her lips parted on a breath. "Don't lie to me, Jay. Don't I deserve the truth?"

"It's the truth," he said calmly, knowing it would take a while for her to understand.

"Are you saying you're a psychic?"

"We don't really call it that. I'm a precognitive. I see future events, almost always visions of doom, of terrible events, just like I saw Dirk."

She furrowed her brows. "You saw him in a vision? Showing up here with a gun?"

"I did. But it didn't end there. I saw the shooting. I saw the people who died, and recognized Grace from a picture you have in your cottage. You'd invited me to the wedding as your date. That's why I knew where it would take place."

"Who died in your vision?" He noticed her lips tremble. "My sister and her husband? Dirk killed them both?"

Jay shook his head. "Her husband survived. Grace didn't. Neither did the two people who they danced with." He met Olivia's gaze. "I couldn't let that happen. You would have lost everybody in your life. Everybody you love."

Olivia's eyes widened. She didn't move, didn't speak, only swallowed hard, before she took a breath. "Dirk killed Grace and my parents?" She blinked her eyes shut for a moment, before looking back at him. "My parents encouraged Grace to get a restraining order against him. For a while, she even moved back in with them, because she didn't feel safe. Dirk must have found out."

It made sense why Dirk had targeted them too and not just Grace. "I'm sorry, Olivia. But it's over now. I was able to prevent it. And Dirk won't be back. My friend and I will make sure of that. I promise you that." He inhaled. "I have to leave. Can I trust you to keep my secret?"

"You can't just leave now."

"I can't stay. I've risked too much already."

Olivia put her hand on his forearm. "You haven't told me anything yet. Who are you really? And don't tell me you're a yoga instructor. Because the way you took down Dirk, the way you handled yourself, that's not something you learn in yoga. Where did you learn this? You knew Dirk had a gun, and from what I can see you're not even armed. You went up against him with your bare hands."

Jay closed his eyes. He wanted to shake off her hand, and ignore her questions, but being near her did something to him. He wanted her to know that he wasn't a bad guy, even though he'd betrayed her trust.

"Jay, please, talk to me."

Slowly, he opened his eyes and looked at her. "Just by being here with you, I'm putting you in danger. You should run as far away from me as you can."

"I can't do that, Jay. I need to know who you are. Damn it, Jay, we made love, and you can't just pretend it meant nothing to you."

"It didn't," he lied, knowing that it was the only way she would let him go.

She shook her head, scoffing. "So you risk your life to save the families of all your one-night stands from armed stalkers? I don't buy it."

Apparently, his skill to lie convincingly wasn't as sharp anymore. Or Olivia's bullshit detector was first rate.

"All right. You win. But before I can give you an answer to your questions, I have to ask you something."

"What do you want to know?"

He watched her face closely, drawing on everything he'd learned at the CIA to help him spot a lie should Olivia not answer him truthfully. "How many of the guests at the wedding do you know?"

"Hmm? Why, uh, what's that got to do with anything?"

"Just answer the question."

"Okay. Well, my parents and sister, and her husband, of course."

"Who else?"

"The bridesmaids, though they're really Grace's friends, but I know them from a few girls' nights out. Why?"

"How about the groom's family? Brothers? Parents? Uncles?"

Olivia shook her head, her forehead furrowing, attesting to the fact that she had no idea why he was asking. "I've met them all for the first time today. And when I say *met* I mean we just exchanged greetings and a little small talk."

"Do you know any other people who are attending the wedding? Any friends or colleagues? Particularly any white men in their fifties or sixties."

"No, I already told you that I don't know anybody. It's all Timothy's friends and family.

And I'm certainly not interested in old white men."

Jay studied her face. He detected no duplicity in her eyes or her manners. She was telling the truth.

"Thank you. I believe you." He paused for a moment, before continuing, "I didn't train in the military. I trained at the Farm."

"The Farm?" she asked.

He didn't answer. Instead, he allowed the news to sink in, so Olivia could draw her own conclusion.

"The CIA?"

He nodded.

"That's why you're disguised, and why you took Dirk down so easily. Your friend too. You're both in the CIA."

"We were," Jay corrected her.

"You quit the CIA?"

Jay contemplated how much to tell her. He knew that Ace's, Fox's, and Yankee's girlfriends knew every detail of what had happened to the former Stargate agents, but Olivia wasn't his girlfriend. He couldn't justify telling her secrets that weren't his alone. He had to protect his fellow agents.

"That's all I can tell you about what I did. I hope you can trust me when I tell you that it's safer for you if you don't know too much. I know that trusting me after I searched your home won't come easy, but I hope you find it within yourself to... believe me just this once."

He looked into her eyes, begging her to understand him.

"You want me to trust you? I can do that. But only if you can explain to me what you were looking for in my office." She tipped her chin up. "I'm assuming now that it wasn't my manuscript."

He shook his head. "No, I really had no idea that you were a famous sci-fi writer. I wasn't there to look for your manuscript. I was looking for evidence that you are connected to a man I'm looking for."

"What man?"

"A white man in his late fifties or early sixties, who goes by the name of Smith, though it's in all likelihood only an alias."

Olivia blinked, catching on quickly. "That's why you asked me whether I knew any of the wedding guests. But why would you even think that I know him?"

"I saw him in your cottage." He took off his glasses, put them on the desk, and rubbed the bridge of his nose.

"When? I haven't had any older men visiting me there. Only my dad, and he's Japanese, not white, and you know that."

"I had a premonition about him entering your cottage. At first, I didn't know that it was your place, but during the vision I saw a photo, and I recognized you from the yoga class. It's the only lead I had on Smith. I needed to follow it, so I had to find out if you knew who he was. But I couldn't just ask you. I had no idea if you were related, or friends, or colleagues, or anything else. So I had to... to get close to you."

Her chin dropped, and for a moment, he had no idea how she would react. "You slept with me just to—"

"No!" he interrupted immediately. "I slept with you because I wanted you from the first moment you set foot in my class."

"If that were true, you would have asked me

out much earlier, and not waited until you thought I could lead you to this man, to Smith."

He ran a hand through his fake hair. "Damn it, I didn't ask you out because I'm ten years older than you, and I have no right to drag a woman I care about into my fucked-up life."

"Goddamn it, Jay! I don't know what to believe anymore." She glared at him.

"Believe this," he said and pulled her into his arms. He captured her lips, before she could protest, and kissed her. For a second, Olivia was stiff in his arms, but then she responded—not by pushing him back like he'd assumed, but by wrapping her arms around him and kissing him back.

He'd missed her, missed feeling her body pressed to his, her lips on his. As much as he wanted to strip her of her dress and bury his aching cock in her, his conscience reared its head, and he severed the kiss. He had to stop himself before he did something irresponsible.

18

Olivia felt cool air waft against her lips, and felt Jay pull away from her.

"I'm sorry, Olivia. I shouldn't be doing this. I shouldn't be dragging you into this mess. Believe me: I only wanted to save your family from the gunman and then disappear without you ever knowing what would have happened. Without you ever seeing me."

"But I saw you. And I can't unsee what you did. You saved my family." And she would always be grateful for that.

But now she had hope for something else too. Jay had said that he'd wanted her from the moment he'd seen her in class. And the feeling was mutual. Maybe there could still be something between them. If she could understand why finding this man was so important to him that it was worth going behind her back, then maybe she could forgive him for that.

"Jay, tell me why you want to find this man so badly that you—"

"That I hurt you in the process?" Jay interrupted and stroked his thumb over her bottom lip. "What difference does it make? I hurt you. I betrayed your trust."

"You strike me as a man who would never do anything unless he had a good reason. Tell me your reason," she begged. "You owe me that for using me."

He nodded slowly. "The man I'm looking for killed my friends, and my mentor, the man I worked for at the CIA. Smith killed him over three years ago, and I've been running for my life ever since."

Olivia sucked in a breath. "Oh my God. He's a murderer? And you thought I was connected to him? How could you even bear to touch me, suspecting that I knew him?"

"It was simple. I didn't want to believe it. I wanted to prove to myself that you had nothing to do with him and knew nothing of his crimes." He sighed. "And yet, you led me to him."

"What?" She shrank back. "But I told you I don't know the man you describe. I ..." Then it suddenly dawned on her. "You asked me if I knew a wedding guest who matched that description. Are you saying that man is here? Right now?"

"I saw him just before I took down Dirk. He was among the guests watching your sister dance."

"Oh my God, you have to call the police. Get him arrested."

"I can't. He can't know that I'm onto him, or that I'm here. Or he'll kill me too."

"But the police, they can protect you."

Jay simply shook his head. "The CIA itself couldn't protect us. There were about thirty of us. All highly skilled, highly trained agents, and Smith managed to wipe us out. I have no idea how many are still alive. I know of several who were killed, most others are in hiding, or dead, I don't know which. I met three fellow agents in the last two weeks. The man who carted Dirk off is one of them."

"But what are you gonna do if you can't go to the police or the CIA?"

"We're looking for him, so we can figure out who he really is, and who he works for. But we've come up empty so far. Unfortunately, we don't have a photo we can run through facial recognition. It's been hampering our search."

"Hold it. You said you saw Smith at the reception. So you know what he looks like, but you don't have a photo?"

"He had me in his clutches almost three weeks ago. The other three agents managed to free me, but Smith escaped."

Olivia's heart pounded. "That's why you skipped class."

"Yeah, and if I hadn't had the premonition of seeing Smith in your cottage, I wouldn't have come back to Alexandria."

Olivia put her arms around him and squeezed him tightly, before she lifted her face up to him, an idea blooming in her mind. "I took photos during cocktail hour in the garden." She pulled her cell phone from her tiny handbag. "Maybe he's on there. I mean there were lots of older white men, not that I really looked. I'm more into"—she smirked—"handsome young black men."

Jay kissed her on the lips. "Excellent idea." Then he smiled at her. "So you think I'm handsome."

Olivia unlocked her cell phone and navigated to her camera app. "As if you don't know that. But if I may make a suggestion: lose the hair. All of it."

"I think that can be arranged."

Together they scrolled through the photos she'd taken in the garden of the hotel. It took Jay only a minute to go through them and shake his head. "He's not on any of them. It was a long shot, but thanks for trying."

Even though he smiled at her, she saw his disappointment. "You know the wedding reception isn't over yet. Most of the guests are still here, dancing and drinking. The band is supposed to play until midnight. I could take more photos."

He stared at her, appearing stunned. "You would do that? For me? Why?"

"Do you really need to ask that?" She brushed her knuckles over his cheek. "You saved my family today. The least I can do is take a few selfies with some of the guests." Then she hesitated. "Smith won't suspect anything, or try to hurt somebody here tonight, will he?"

Jay instantly shook his head. "He has no reason to. And he's not careless. He wouldn't expose himself. Besides, everybody is taking photos at a wedding. There's nothing suspicious about it." He took her hands into his. "But you don't have to do it if you feel uncomfortable. I won't be able to go down there with you."

"I know that. You just wait here, while I mingle. My parents are probably wondering anyway where I am. I might be a couple of hours. Will you be okay here?"

He nodded. "Do you have your computer here?"

His question sent a shock through her system. "Uhm…"

"Sorry," he said quickly. "Believe me, I'm really not after your manuscript."

"I'm sorry, it's just a habit. But I didn't bring my computer. It's locked in my safe at home. Why do you need it?"

"I figure if you take pictures with your cell phone, I can log into your cloud and look at the pictures in real time, and let you know when you can stop."

"Oh, good idea." Then she turned to her travel bag. "You can do the same on my tablet. It's synched with my cell."

"Perfect," Jay said and took the tablet she handed him. "Passcode?"

She typed the six-digit number in slowly, so he could memorize it.

"Thank you." Then he laid the tablet on the bed and pulled her into his arms. "Just be your normal self at the reception. Dance with a few guys. You have to look like you're having fun."

"I wish I could have fun with you."

Jay chuckled. "Would it help to know that

when you come back to your room, we could talk about having fun?"

"Just talk?"

He let his hand slide down to her backside, drawing her closer to him. "That'll be up to you. Now, go. I'll send you a text if I see something of concern on the photos."

She lifted herself on her tiptoes and kissed him. "Okay. I'll see you soon."

Olivia left the room, a multitude of feelings colliding inside her: gratitude, shock, relief, and yes, even fear, because the fact that the man hunting Jay was a guest at the wedding reception sent fear into her bones. But she tried to suppress that particular feeling, because Jay needed her help, and just like he'd taken an enormous risk in order to save her sister and her parents, she could certainly do this little thing for him. How hard could it be to take a few photos at a wedding?

When Olivia entered the ballroom and glanced around, she saw her father dancing with her mother. Seeing them happy and healthy made her choke up all of a sudden, and she approached them. Her mother saw her first and looked at her.

"Honey, where were you? Everything all right?" she asked.

Olivia put her arms around both her parents and smiled. "Everything is perfect. I'm so happy you guys are here. I wish you didn't have to fly back so soon."

Her mother gave her a kiss on the cheek. "So do we."

"How about a dance with your old father, Olivia?" her father asked, releasing her mother.

"You're not old, Dad. And who's Mom gonna dance with?"

"Oh, don't worry about me," she said laughing. "I see a few handsome young men who don't seem to have a dance partner."

Her father smirked and took Olivia's hand, before he pulled her into his arms and started dancing. It had been a long time since she'd danced, but it was like riding a bike, and with her father leading expertly, it was a breeze.

"You look so much happier now," her father remarked. "I was a little worried about you earlier." Sometimes her father was just a little too perceptive.

"I'm fine, Dad." She smiled at him. "Just some worries about the book. Some rumors that have been going around about the book that had me worried. It's all sorted out."

"Well, good. And you shouldn't constantly be thinking about work. You're young, you're beautiful. And I've noticed plenty of men here looking at you. Enjoy yourself a little."

"I *am* enjoying myself, Dad," she protested.

He chuckled, then twirled her one last time and released her right in front of a thirty-something guy. "Young man, can you take this woman off my hands, please? I'm in no condition to dance anymore."

"Of course, sir!" The guy beamed.

Olivia shot her father an annoyed look. There was nothing wrong with her father's condition. He still surfed almost daily.

He winked at her, and Olivia had no choice but to dance and make pleasant conversation with the man. Luckily, the band announced a short break just after their dance ended, and Olivia was able to shake off her dance partner.

Finally, she would be able to take photos. She glanced around to search for any white guy over forty, when she caught sight of her sister, who was speaking to Timothy. The groom didn't look very happy, and a moment later, he disappeared among the guests.

When Olivia noticed her sister's sad expression, she hurried over to her. "Grace?" She put her hand on her sister's arm. "Is something wrong? I just saw Timothy—"

"Nothing to worry about, sis," Grace said quickly. "Tim is upset because his mother left already. She couldn't even be bothered to stay halfway through the evening."

Olivia sighed. "Let me guess: she saw how happy her ex-husband is with his new wife and couldn't stand being here?"

"Probably. Maybe we should have just eloped to spare everybody the family drama." Then she smiled. "Don't worry. Tim just needs to take a breather. He'll be fine."

Olivia put her arms around her sister and squeezed her. "I love you, sis."

"I love you, too. Now go, have fun. Did I just

see you dance with one of Tim's college buddies?"

Olivia rolled her eyes. "Dad ambushed me."

Grace chuckled. "It worked when he did that for me. Or I might have never met Tim."

"I'm perfectly happy right now," she said and meant it. After all, she had a handsome hunk waiting for her in her hotel room. "I should take a few photos with everybody here so I'll have something to remember this day."

Just then, Timothy returned, and put his arm around his bride. "Sorry, baby." He kissed her, then looked at Olivia. "Hey, sis! You owe me a dance."

"Band's on a break," Olivia said.

Timothy grinned. "Not for long. So don't go anywhere."

"I promise, but I might as well take pictures while we're waiting."

She pulled out her cell phone and went to work.

19

Jay contacted Yankee, giving him a brief update about his search for Smith and how Olivia was helping him, so the guys at the mansion wouldn't get worried if they didn't get word from him for a few hours. It was close to midnight when Jay heard a sound at the door. Somebody was using a keycard to unlock it. He jumped up from the bed, where he'd been lounging while looking through the photos that Olivia had sent to the cloud over the last few hours. Remaining quiet, he pressed himself against a wall, where he couldn't be seen by the person opening the door.

The door opened, then fell shut a few seconds later, when the person entering reached his field of vision.

"Jay?"

Jay let out a breath and moved.

Olivia gasped and pressed her hand to her chest. "You startled me."

"Sorry," he said. "Old habits die hard."

"Did you get all the photos?"

He nodded.

"And? Is Smith among them?"

"I'm afraid not. Are you sure you got a photo of every man fitting his description?"

"Everybody who was there, yes. This was all for nothing?" She plopped down on the bed and pulled off her shoes. "My feet are killing me."

Jay crouched down to her feet. "I'm sorry that it was a bust." He took one foot into his hand and began massaging it. "I'm grateful for what you've done for me."

"Oh, that feels good," she murmured.

"Just relax now. You deserve it."

She dropped her head toward his. "You know what would really relax me?"

"What's that?"

She kissed him below his ear, then whispered, "You making love to me."

Jay let out a breath. He wanted nothing more than to feel Olivia in his arms, his cock buried deep inside her, but his conscience didn't allow him to act on it, because there was still something he hadn't confessed.

He rose to his feet and pulled a chair closer. When he sat down on it, Olivia gave him an odd look. "Is something wrong? You don't want to have sex with me?"

"I want nothing more, but I can't, because there's something I haven't told you yet. And you're not gonna like it."

Her breath hitched. "What is it?"

"The night we had sex for the first time, I got up in the middle of the night and installed surveillance equipment in your home, cameras and recording devices."

Olivia gasped and jumped up. "Oh my God! How could you? You were filming me?"

Jay rose. "I'm sorry. I had no choice. I need to capture Smith when he shows up at your place, because he will. My premonitions are never wrong."

"So you violated my privacy? You recorded everything I did?"

"I didn't install any cameras in the bedroom or the bathroom. But yes, I violated your privacy. And you have every right to be angry with me."

"Angry? You think I'm angry? I'm furious! Why didn't you tell me about this earlier when you told me about everything else? Why keep this from me?"

He cast his gaze to the floor. "Because despite everything you told me tonight, despite you reassuring me that you didn't know Smith—"

"Which is the truth!"

"I know that. But Smith captured me once before, and did horrendous things to me. I couldn't tell you about the bugs in your house. If you'd come back here tonight leading Smith to me—"

Olivia let out a gasp. "You thought I would sell you out?"

"No, I didn't. But there was a chance that

you could inadvertently lead him to me. And if Smith managed to kill me, then at least the bugs weren't compromised. My friends would still have a chance to record Smith when he shows up in your cottage."

"Then why would you even show up here to save my family? And why risk waiting here for me when you thought I could lead that murderer to you?"

Jay looked into her eyes. "Because I'm in love with you, Olivia."

He noticed Olivia's surprise, her lips parting, but he didn't give her a chance to say anything. He needed to get all of it off his chest.

"I had no choice when it came to whether to save your family or not. I couldn't bear the thought of you losing everybody you love. And later, when you offered to help me identify him, I had to stay here to make sure you were all right in case Smith was still at the reception and got suspicious of you when you were taking photos. You don't know what Smith is capable of, but he's an evil man. The things he does, the things he's planning..."

Jay shook his head. He didn't want to think back to how he'd felt when Smith had put him into the machine to scan his brain. But he had to explain to Olivia why he'd done what he'd done.

"I have to get to Smith, no matter the cost. Even if that means that you hate me and will never let me touch you again. But he has to be stopped, or he'll do to others what he did to me."

"You said he's a murderer. Then why didn't he kill you, when he captured you?"

"I'm no use to him dead. He needs what's in here." He tapped at his temple.

"Secret information?"

Jay shook his head. "He built a machine to capture that part of my brain that's responsible for my premonitions. He's already done it to one of the other agents, and possibly to several more. He's trying to build a quantum computer capable of spitting out one hundred percent accurate predictions of future events, and he needs what's in my brain and that of the other agents who have the same gift as I."

"You mean there are other CIA agents who have premonitions like you?"

He nodded. "Yes, we were all in the same program. And Smith is hunting us."

"And Smith managed to extract whatever he needed from your brain?"

"No. My friends saved me in time. If he'd succeeded, I wouldn't be here anymore. The process fries the brain, turns it to mush. Nobody can survive it."

Tears suddenly welled up in Olivia's eyes. "Oh my God." She made a step toward him. "Jay, I can't imagine what you've been through." She shook her head and put a hand on his arm. "And I'm worried about you stealing my manuscript and filming me in my home? You must think I'm silly and self-absorbed, when you have real problems."

"I'm so sorry, Olivia. Please forgive me."

"Jay? Did you mean what you said earlier when you said..." She hesitated.

"I meant everything I said." Though he wasn't sure what exactly she was referring to.

"You said you're in love with me. Is that true?" She gazed into his eyes.

Instinctively, he reached for her and slid his arm around her waist. "Yes, it's true, even though I have no right to ask you to be with me..."

"Why not?"

"I'm on the run, Olivia. And you have a career, a family, far too much to give up. How could I ask that of you?" He smiled at her despite the pain in his heart.

He couldn't ask her to give up her existing life to live in hiding with him, no matter how much he wanted to. But he also couldn't ignore his premonition of Smith showing up in Olivia's cottage. What would happen when Smith showed up in her home? He'd only seen a snippet of the event. He had no idea whether he would hurt her, or if there was a way to prevent Smith from ever showing up in Olivia's home in the first place. If there was a way to prevent this premonition from coming true, he couldn't figure it out right now. He needed to clear his head.

Olivia seemed to understand instinctively that he wasn't ready to have that discussion. "Let's talk about it tomorrow. I always do my best plotting in the morning." She pressed herself to him. "How about you take that disguise off?"

"So you really don't like the hair, huh?"

"The beard itches when you kiss me."

He laughed softly. "So, we're gonna kiss?"

"Among other things..."

"Which are?"

"Why don't you get undressed, so I can show you?"

20

Minutes later, Jay hadn't only rid himself of the beard and wig, but also of his clothes. Olivia was naked too, and he couldn't get enough of looking at her perfect body and creamy skin. He made a step toward her to pull her into his arms, but Olivia dropped to her knees in front of him.

"Oh, fuck!" he cursed, realizing what she was planning. "I haven't touched you in two days, and you wanna start off with a blow job? You know what that's gonna do to me?"

She lifted her lids and cast him a sinful

smile. "Oh, I sure hope so. Now be good and sit on the edge of the bed so I can suck you."

He followed her command and sat down, spreading his thighs. His cock hung between his legs, hard and heavy, waiting for her touch, while he breathed hard. He'd never been so aroused simply by looking at a naked woman, but knowing that sweet, forgiving Olivia was eager to take his cock into her mouth despite everything he'd done, made his pulse race.

Olivia wrapped one hand around the root of his cock, sending a shockwave through his body. A gasp escaped him, but before he could catch his breath, her lips were already wrapping around the tip of his erection, and her tongue was licking over it.

"Fuck, baby," Jay let out and put his hands on her shoulders.

Slowly, Olivia took him deep into her mouth, until he could descend no farther. Her warmth and wetness robbed him of his ability to think. Every sane thought he'd ever had in his life vanished into nothingness. Only the here and now counted, only this moment of sheer and utter bliss. As if only the two of them existed.

Like a skilled temptress, Olivia slid down on his cock again and again, her saliva lubricating him, her hand around the base adding just the right pressure to stop him from coming instantly. Where had she learned how to suck him with such expert skill? Almost as if she'd taken lessons so she could seduce him to do anything she wanted him to do. Because the way she sucked him now, the way she pleasured him, he knew he could never deny her anything. He looked down at her body, and saw the perspiration that built on her skin, and the rosy flush that spread over her entire body. The contrast of her pale skin to his own, much darker one, was stark, yet perfect. As if made for each other, the yin and the yang.

All of a sudden, Olivia sucked him harder and faster, and he knew he couldn't allow her to continue, or he would come in her mouth, and while he hoped to satisfy that erotic fantasy with her at some point, right now, he wanted nothing more than to feel her pussy cradle his cock.

"Enough!" he demanded and pulled himself out of Olivia's mouth.

She looked up at him, her expression almost innocent, yet her lips betraying that innocence. They were red and plump, and he'd never seen anything more erotic. He pulled her up and took her lips, kissing her hard, until they were both breathless. Meanwhile, he gripped her hips and pulled her onto his lap, so she straddled him, his cock sliding against her pussy. He shifted his angle, until she gasped. He'd found the right spot, and was now rubbing his cock over her clitoris.

He let go of her lips, and Olivia arched her back, pressing her clit harder against his cock, while offering her breasts to him. Holding her with both arms slung around her waist, so she couldn't slip from his lap, he let her ride his cock without penetrating her, while he began sucking her breasts.

"Fuck, I love your tits," he murmured as he sucked one nipple between his lips.

Olivia moaned. "I'm so close. So close."

He brought his hands to her hips, assisting

her as she rode him faster, while still allowing her to set her own rhythm.

"You're so beautiful," he whispered. "I'm gonna fuck you all night, baby, you hear me? All night."

"Tell me more."

Did Olivia get turned on by dirty talk? If that's what she needed, he had no problem giving it to her.

"I'm gonna sink my cock into your sweet pussy, deep and hard. I'm gonna take you so long that you won't be able to breathe. Is that what you want? Me taking you like a beast?" Like he'd done when he'd taken her in the foyer of her cottage.

"Yes! Yes!" A shudder went through her body, and he knew she was climaxing.

He didn't waste a second, lifted her just enough to bring his cock to the entrance of her body and impale her with it. Her pussy was still spasming, clenching around his cock, while he remained inside her but didn't move. Only when her orgasm ebbed, did he begin to move inside her in a slow and steady rhythm.

"So good," she murmured.

Yes, it was good. Better even than the previous times. That's when he realized why.

"Fuck! Olivia, I forgot the condom."

He lifted her to pull himself out of her, but she stopped him. "I'm on the pill. Please don't stop now. I like feeling you like this. Without a barrier."

"Are you sure? I can stop if—" Who was he kidding? He couldn't stop. He wanted this, wanted to be inside her like this, wanted to fill her with his semen as if she was his.

Olivia dictated the tempo with which she moved up and down on him now, using her knees for leverage. Her breasts were bouncing up and down right in front of his face, and he captured one of them and sucked the nipple into his mouth. At the same time, he brought one hand between their bodies and found her clitoris. He let the nipple pop from his mouth.

"Like that?"

"I need you to get deeper," she said on a moan.

He couldn't do that in his current position. He dropped back onto the mattress, then flipped them so Olivia was underneath him now, her legs spread wide, his cock plunging into her, reaching deeper than before.

"That's what you want?"

"Yes! Fuck me with your beautiful big cock."

He rode her, pulling one of her legs up and draping it over his shoulder, spreading her wider, while he thrust slowly, enjoying her interior muscles gripping him like a tight fist.

"Play with your clit," he ordered, because he had no free hand to do it himself and because seeing a woman pleasure herself was an erotic sight he enjoyed.

When Olivia followed his command, he praised her, "Good girl."

She looked at him, her eyes full of love and desire, and he knew that even if he met his death tomorrow or the day after, he'd die a happy man, because Olivia looked at him the way he felt about her. The knowledge that she wanted him and trusted him like nobody before sent him over the edge. He couldn't hold back his orgasm, his cock already jerking inside her, releasing its seed.

"Yes, Jay," she murmured and arched her back, climaxing a few seconds after him.

His heart was pounding, bliss engulfing him, and on the horizon he saw something that looked like hope. Maybe what was between them was strong enough after all.

As his orgasm ebbed, with Olivia stilled beneath him, he brought his lips to hers. "I've never felt so good in my entire life." He kissed her softly, the need for tenderness rising in him now. "Thank you for forgiving me."

She slid her hand onto his nape, caressing him. "I can't be mad at you for something that you did to survive. And when you make love to me like this, it's even harder to hold a grudge."

"I'll keep that in mind." He smirked. "So you like to rob me of my self-control, don't you? Like you did when I took you in the foyer of your cottage?"

"Yes, you got me so—" She suddenly let out a gasp and he lifted his head to give her space. "Oh no, the foyer! You said you put a camera there. Does that mean there's a sex tape of us out there?"

"No, there isn't. I erased it."

"You did?"

"Yes, before any of the other agents could see it. Trust me, I don't want a sex tape of you out there for other men to watch. I don't want anybody but me to see you like this."

A smile formed on her lips. "And I don't want any other women to see you like this either." She slid one hand onto his ass and pressed him to her, making his cock slide deeper into her again. "I don't like to share."

"Me neither."

21

Olivia snuggled closer against the warm body spooning her and felt something hard sliding against her backside. She recognized what it was: Jay's cock. He was hard again despite the fact that they'd made love twice before they'd both fallen asleep.

She shifted in his arms, until his cock slipped between her thighs.

"You're insatiable," Jay whispered into her ear.

"You're awake."

"Mmmhmm."

He gripped her thigh and lifted it, then

slowly drove his cock into her pussy. She welcomed the invasion and reached for Jay's hand, pulling it to her breasts. She loved the way he was able to arouse her instantly. He began to gently thrust in and out of her, while he caressed her breasts just as tenderly. Last night he'd taken her much more urgently, but this morning, every touch and every thrust was infused with tenderness.

"I love the way you touch me," she whispered.

"Because I love touching you." He continued thrusting into her, but didn't increase his tempo, drawing out the pleasure. "Every time you were in class and I came to adjust your yoga poses, I wanted to take you into my arms..." He moaned softly. "It was torture."

"We'll just have to make up for lost time now," Olivia suggested.

Jay brushed her hair aside and kissed her shoulders and neck. "I'm all for that."

He pulled almost completely out of her, before slicing back into her in one continuous movement, his cock filling her tight channel.

"Do that again," she murmured.

"That?" he asked and pulled out until only the bulbous head was still inside her.

"Yes, that." When he drove back into her, she sucked in a breath, and felt her clit throb. It felt as if his cock was touching every cell of her body, setting her on fire.

She was suddenly aware of Jay pinching her nipple and gasped at the erotic sensation that sent an electric charge into her clit.

"Are you always so horny in the morning?" he asked, his hot breath at her neck.

"Look who's talking," she replied breathlessly.

He chuckled and moved his hand down her torso. When he combed through the triangle of hair between her legs, Olivia inhaled, and her pulse drummed faster. Jay stroked over her clit. Her orgasm hit her out of nowhere, and her pussy clenched around his cock. This had never happened to her before, not like this. She normally needed more stimulation.

"Just like I thought," Jay murmured in her ear, before he thrust faster in and out of her.

"You're so hot, baby, you should be fucked twenty-four-seven."

Seconds later, she felt his cock spasm, and a corresponding wetness spread inside her.

"Fuck!"

Olivia chuckled. Apparently, she wasn't the only one who was horny this morning.

"You little minx." He kissed her shoulder. "Let's take a shower and get dressed, before you take advantage of me again."

"Would that be so bad?" She turned to look at him.

"Don't tempt me."

Jay jumped out of bed, and Olivia followed him. Together they showered and got dressed. As Olivia combed her wet hair, she had an idea.

"Jay?"

He appeared in the bathroom door, the fake beard and wig in his hands. "Yes?"

"I was thinking about Smith. Since you saw him at the reception when you took down Dirk, he would have been there earlier too, during the cocktail hour."

"What are you trying to say?"

"He would have been here when the photographer took the group photos. We should look at those photos."

"Do you have them already?"

"No, but I can talk to the photographer, and have him send them to me. I dealt with him when I helped Grace organize all the vendors for the wedding. He knows me, and I'm sure he'll have no trouble sending me the proofs before he's done touching them up."

Jay pressed a kiss to her lips. "That's a genius idea."

"See? I told you I have my best ideas in the morning."

He smirked. "Oh, I've been at the receiving end of your ideas this morning." He snaked his arm around her and pulled her to him.

"You have a—"

A knock at the door interrupted her. They exchanged a look.

"Housekeeping?" Jay whispered over the sound of the bathroom's exhaust fan.

"Probably."

"Tell her to come back later," he said, and

Olivia left the bathroom and pulled the door shut behind her.

She opened the room door, ready to send the maid away, when she realized that it wasn't the maid who'd knocked, but her parents. Crap!

"Ah, Mom, Dad, what—"

"Did you oversleep?" her father asked, while her mother already squeezed past her into the room. Her father entered the room too, and Olivia let the door fall shut.

"You haven't even packed yet, Olivia," her mother chastised her softly. "The reservation is for noon. We'd better hurry."

That's when she remembered. She'd promised her parents to go to lunch with them at *Fiola Mare* in the Foggy Bottom neighborhood of D.C. It was one of their favorite places when they'd lived in Virginia.

"Oh, yeah, uh, I guess I had a little much to drink last night. How about I get packed and then meet you downstairs in the lobby?"

Her mother made a dismissive hand movement. "It'll be faster if I help you."

"Mom, that's not necessary."

But she couldn't be dissuaded, and already lifted Olivia's leather travel bag onto the bed.

Olivia shot a pleading look at her father. "Dad, can you just—"

But her father shrugged. "I try not to interfere when your mother decides on doing something." Then he turned toward the bathroom door, and added, "Let me just use your bathroom."

Before she could stop him, he was already opening the door. He froze, then glanced back at Olivia. "Why didn't you say you had company?"

"Company?" her mother asked and approached.

Jay, dressed in black pants and a white shirt, disguised with his fake beard and wig, stepped out of the bathroom. "Uh, good morning. The sink is fixed, ma'am, sir."

But he wasn't fooling anybody. Her mother gave him a curious look, and her father smirked.

"Honey, if you'd told me what your type was," her father said with a grin, "I wouldn't have wasted your time to get you to dance with all those guys last night."

"Sam, stop it," her mother said quickly. "Can't you see that you're embarrassing them?" Then she extended her hand toward Jay. "I'm Alice Morikawa. And you are?"

Jay took her hand and shook it. "Jay, Jay, uh, Zurich."

Olivia noticed the slight hesitation when he said his last name and guessed that the last name he had used at the yoga studio, and was now giving her mother, was as fake as his beard. She wasn't surprised.

As Jay shook hands with her mother, and then her father, Olivia addressed her parents, "Why don't I meet you down in the lobby in half an hour? And then the three of us can go to lunch."

"Maybe Jay would like to join us for lunch," her father suggested.

"That's very kind," Jay said quickly, "but I've got an appointment in downtown D.C. I'd better go get a cab."

"We can drop you off in D.C. We're heading

that way anyway," her father suggested. "We'll meet in twenty minutes in the lobby?"

Olivia exchanged a look with Jay. "Sure, we'll see you downstairs."

The moment the door shut behind her parents, Olivia let out a sigh. "Damn it, I totally forgot that I was supposed to have lunch with them. They're flying back to Hawaii tonight. It's really the only time I get to see them."

Jay cast her a smile. "Go for lunch with them. I'll have them drop me off at one of the Metro stations in D.C., and when you're done with lunch, we'll go over the group photos. Can you contact the photographer now so he can email you the photos, and you'll have them by the time you're done with lunch?"

"Yes, I can do that. I hope I can reach him. I'll text you when lunch is over and when I've got the photos."

"You don't have my number."

"I do. You gave it to me the other day."

"That number is dead already." He pulled his phone from his pocket. "I'll text you my new number."

When her phone pinged, Jay put his fingers

under Olivia's chin to make her look at him. "And, Olivia, don't tell your parents anything about me. I know they'll ask, but don't tell them that you know me from your yoga class. Just say that I'm a hotel guest. Just a one-night stand. It's safer for them."

Olivia nodded. "You're lucky that my parents are free spirits and don't condemn one-night stands."

"I doubt they could stop you even if they disapproved." Jay smiled and pressed a kiss to her lips.

22

It was close to 3 p.m. when Jay met up with Olivia at a café not far from the White House. It was packed with tourists. He'd bought a baseball cap, sunglasses, and a Washington D.C. T-shirt in a tourist shop, and now blended in with the tourists visiting the nation's capital. Even Olivia walked past him, when she entered the café, looking for him.

When she finally saw him, she smiled and sat down at the tiny bistro table and set her travel bag beneath it. Jay leaned in and kissed her briefly on the lips. "How was lunch with your parents?"

"It was wonderful." She chuckled. "And you were right; they wanted to know more about you. But I stuck to the story."

"Good." Then he pushed one of the cups of coffee in front of him toward her. "You don't have to drink it. It's just so you have a drink in front of you." He didn't want them to stick out in any way. "Did the photographer get back to you?"

"Yes, he sent me the photos." She leaned down and pulled her tablet from her travel bag and unlocked it.

Jay moved his chair closer to her and put his arm around her. He cast furtive looks around him, but none of the tourists was interested in them. He looked into the screen as Olivia tapped on an email and opened the attachments.

"Here we go," she said.

There were several photos of the wedding guests lined up on the stairs leading from the back of the hotel into the large garden. The bride and groom were standing in the front flanked by the bridesmaids. The other guests stood behind them on higher steps, so the camera could capture their faces. Jay looked at every man on the first photo, then moved on to the next.

"Anything?" Olivia asked after he'd looked at the first three photos.

He shook his head and continued examining the photos. There were more photos, some of them more informal, some of them probably taken by the photographer to check the lighting and set up the correct shot. In those shots, the guests were moving around, many of them not looking at the camera, but talking to their neighbors.

"There," he said and pointed to one of the guests. The man pictured had turned away from the other guests. The camera had only captured his back. "He avoided the camera. He didn't want to be in the photos. He's careful." He looked at Olivia and gave her a regretful smile. "That's a dead end."

Olivia sighed and switched off the tablet. "I wish I could have helped you."

"You did." He kissed her on the cheek. "I'll figure out something else."

Olivia sipped on the coffee he'd gotten her,

then set the cup down and stared at him, a glint of excitement in her eyes. "I might have another idea."

"Of how to identify him?"

"Yes. I helped my sister with the guest list, and then handled all the RSVPs. I have the names of all the guests. If we could somehow cross-reference the names to pictures, we could cross off the names of people that we can match to photos from the wedding."

"Or their driver's licenses," Jay added, having an idea of how to identify all guests.

"But how would you get their—" Olivia stopped herself, and leaned closer, dropping her voice to a whisper. "You mean you can hack into the DMV?"

"I can't, but I know somebody who can." Fox or Michelle could do that. "Is the guest list on your tablet?"

She shook her head. "No, only on my computer at home."

"Okay, let's go to your place and get your computer."

Jay took Olivia's travel bag and stood up. Together they left the café.

"I can call us an Uber," Olivia suggested.

"An Uber can be traced back to you, and eventually to me. I have a better idea. Here, wear this." He reached into his back pocket and pulled out a second baseball cap he'd bought and handed it to Olivia.

She took it and put it on. "Okay."

"And put your sunglasses on."

As they walked, Jay pulled out his cell phone and redialed the last number.

Ace answered the call. "Where are you?"

"Still downtown. We're heading to Olivia's house. The photos were a bust."

"He's probably too smart to get caught on camera."

"I figured as much, but Olivia came up with another idea. We just need to get her laptop, and then we'll be heading your way. Watch my back."

"Yankee is watching the cottage on the monitors. It's all clear."

"See you." He disconnected the call.

"How are we getting to Alexandria? The Metro?" Olivia asked.

"No. This way," he said and ushered her

into a small parking lot with an electronic pay station. There was no parking attendant. Jay glanced around to find a suitable car, something common that wouldn't attract attention.

He found it quickly, then glanced around to make sure that nobody was watching.

"What are you doing?" Olivia asked.

"Getting us a ride to Alexandria." Jay pulled out his cellphone and navigated to an app that Fox had installed for him a few days earlier. He leaned over the windshield of the white Toyota Corolla and scanned the VIN. Moments later, a series of beeps sounded, then the familiar click of car doors unlocking.

"That's not your car, is it?" Olivia asked, looking worried.

"It is for now. Don't worry, I don't intend to keep it." He opened the car door and lifted the travel bag on the backseat. "Get in." He waited until Olivia opened the passenger door, before getting in himself.

"Switch off your cell phone. We don't want anybody to be able to track you," Jay said, and Olivia did as he demanded.

It took him all of thirty seconds to hotwire the car, and moments later, they were on the road, driving through Washington D.C. Jay cast a sideways look at Olivia and noticed that she still looked worried.

"Relax, I know what I'm doing. This is not the first time I've done this."

"I figured that much from how easy you made it look. I suppose that app on your phone isn't something anybody can download from the app store."

"You'd be surprised..." He put his hand on hers and squeezed it. "Do you regret not having tossed me out of your room last night after you realized what kind of life I live?"

Olivia took an audible breath. "No, I don't regret it. But I'm still trying to adjust to all this... stealing cars, planting surveillance devices, and all that spy stuff." Then she suddenly let out a laugh. "If I ever wrote something like this in one of my books, my editor would cross it out and tell me to write something more believable."

Jay chuckled. "You write sci-fi. Trust me

there are a lot more unrealistic scenarios in sci-fi than the situation we're in right now."

"Yeah, but in sci-fi I know that it's all made up. This"—she made an all-encompassing motion with her hands—"this is reality. When I'm writing my books, I feel safe, because I can move the action in whatever direction I like. I'm the captain of my ship. But this, this is different."

Jay understood all too well what she was going through. He'd felt like that when Smith had captured him. He'd known exactly what was happening to him, yet he'd been unable to do anything about it to prevent it.

"I wish I could tell you that it'll get better, or that you'll get used to it. You won't. I was trained for this, for being ready for every situation, and still I will never get used to it. Used to being forced to do things that you don't want to do, just to survive. To make choices you'd never make under other circumstances."

"Then how do you do it? How do you do the things you have to do, and not fall apart?"

"I imagine what will happen if I don't do

what I must. They'll catch me and rob me of my mind, and destroy my body. And then they'll do it to others, until they have so much power that they will destroy democracy as we know it, and destroy anybody who dares rise up in protest."

"How do you know that this will happen?"

"Because I've seen it happen. In a recurring premonition I've had for the last three years."

Olivia gasped. "What did you see?"

"I saw how the Capitol building blew up. The shockwave was so strong, so powerful that it slammed me against a metal fence. I was helpless. For a long time, I didn't know what the premonition meant. But when Smith captured me, I found out that by using my gift and that of the other agents to build a quantum computer, he'll soon have all the power he needs to take whatever he wants: money and power. And nobody will be able to stop him. He'll destroy anybody who dares resist."

"Oh my God, you really can't trust anybody."

"Only the guys who saved me from certain

death." And those three men he trusted with his life.

They were just crossing the Woodrow Wilson Memorial Bridge, and Jay moved into the right lane to take the exit into Alexandria, when Jay's phone rang. He pulled it out of his pocket and answered the call.

"Yeah?"

"Tell me you're not at Olivia's house yet," Yankee said, his voice tense.

"We're about ten minutes out."

"Thank God. Divert immediately. Smith just showed up. He's inside the cottage."

"Fuck!" Jay hissed.

"What?" Olivia asked, and Jay put the call on speaker.

"Yankee, Olivia is listening in. What's Smith doing?"

"He's looking around every room. He's not touching anything, but he's checking the place out."

"I have no connection to Smith," Olivia said. "Why the hell would he go into my house?"

"He must have connected you with Tiger

somehow."

"Tiger?"

"That's me," Jay said quickly.

"He must have seen you two together. Maybe after you went back inside the hotel. Otherwise, there's nothing that could tip him off that you two know each other."

Jay took the freeway exit into Alexandria, but didn't drive in the direction of Olivia's house.

"Oh fuck!" Yankee suddenly hissed. "He's installing bugs."

"Crap!" Jay echoed, then looked at Olivia, as he stopped on a quiet side street. "We can't go back to your house, not now while he's still there, and not later either, or he'll have us on camera."

"But my computer!" Olivia protested.

"We won't need it anymore, now that we have Smith on camera. Yankee, we have a good picture of his face, right?" Jay asked.

"Yep. As if he were posing at the DMV. He's in the bag. Now we just need to run facial recognition, and we'll find him."

"Jay, you don't understand," Olivia

interrupted, her voice pleading. "I need my computer and my backup hard drive from my safe. My manuscript is on there, my series bible, my outlines, my character resumes, everything. Jay, that's my life. I need my computer."

"You didn't save your files in the cloud?"

"And have them hacked? Of course not."

Jay took a breath. "Fuck!"

"Hold it, Tiger," Fox suddenly joined the conversation. "I might have a way of scrambling Smith's bugs for a short while to give you a window to go inside, but I'm not sure yet. I have to figure out what kind of bugs he's installing first. Give me a little time. We'll be in touch. In the meantime, stay away from the cottage. We'll text you when he's leaving. Sit tight."

Fox disconnected the call.

23

Olivia was getting more and more anxious. Smith was in her house, installing surveillance equipment, and she couldn't get inside to retrieve her most prized possessions: her manuscript and all that went with it. This was her worst nightmare coming to pass. She was nothing without her work, without her stories. She'd always known that, but she'd never imagined that it would come to this one day.

"But why can't I just go in once Smith leaves, get my stuff and leave? You don't have to go with me," she said.

"If you go in there, and all you do is

retrieve your computer, and leave again immediately, he might suspect that we're onto him. He's no dummy. We're lucky if he doesn't discover that your place is already bugged," Jay said, and took her hand. "We'll figure something out."

"But how can I even live there knowing that Smith is filming everything? I can't do that. I have to move."

"One step at a time, okay? First, we'll wait for Fox to figure out how we can bypass Smith's cameras."

"This Fox, he's one of the agents who saved you, right?"

Jay nodded.

"So he's a precognitive like you. How is that gonna help us get my computer?"

"He's a master when it comes to IT, and his girlfriend is an ex-hacker. She was part of Anonymous, until she got caught and Smith blackmailed her into sniffing out Fox. Long story short, she fell in love with Fox, and turned on Smith. Now they both work on anything IT related that can help us find Smith."

"It's been an hour already. What if neither he nor his girlfriend come up with a solution?"

"Both of them are the best of the best. And together, they're unbeatable. The two of them were able to hack into Langley, and trust me, getting behind the CIA's firewalls is no small feat." He leaned over to her, and pressed a kiss to her lips. "Trust me, Olivia."

She nodded, and put one hand on his nape, pulling him closer. "I do."

She brushed her lips to his as an invitation, and Jay accepted it, and kissed her, his lips firm, his tongue tender and gentle. She knew he would do everything he could to rectify the situation they were in.

Jay's cell phone suddenly rang. He severed the kiss and looked at the display. "That's Fox." He put the call on speaker.

"What have you got for us, Fox?" Jay asked.

"Okay, there is a way for me to take the signal from the surveillance equipment you planted and reverse it so that I can scramble the signal of Smith's bugs. But I can only do it for forty-five seconds, a minute max, or I'll fry his equipment, and he'll know that we're onto him."

Jay tossed her a questioning look. "Can you get your computer out in forty-five seconds?"

Olivia nodded. "It's gonna be tight. The safe is behind a panel in the office closet."

"I'll give you as much time as I can," Fox promised, "but you've gotta hurry. And don't move anything else. When the feed is back, everything has to look exactly like it did before I interrupted his feed. Got it?"

Olivia understood. "I can do it."

"Okay. I'll stay on the line. Tell me when you're at the door to your house, key at the ready."

"And Smith?" Jay asked quickly.

"He left half an hour ago."

"Good," Jay said and started the car's engine. They were only a five-minute drive from her house.

At first, Jay drove right past it, and Olivia said, "You passed it."

"I know. I just want to make sure that nobody is lying in wait. Unfortunately, we don't have any cameras on the outside of your house."

Now she understood. Even though Smith had left half an hour earlier, he could be sitting in a parked car. Olivia let her eyes roam.

"All clear," Jay said and drove around the block, then parked the car on Olivia's block.

As they got out of the car, Jay took his phone from Olivia's hand and spoke into it. "We're almost at the door."

"Standing by," Fox confirmed.

At the door to her home, Olivia pulled her house key from her handbag, before looking at Jay. "I'm ready."

"Fox," Jay said, "you give the signal."

The tapping of a keyboard could be heard from the cell phone. "Put your key in the lock. Unlock on my command."

Olivia put the key in the lock, her heart racing now.

"On three. One, two, three."

Olivia unlocked the door and pushed it inward, then charged into the house. The house was just like she'd left it. Smith hadn't disturbed a single thing. If it weren't for the surveillance equipment Jay had installed, she would have never known that a stranger had been in her house and would be recording her every move.

In the office, she raced to the closet and slid the door to the side, then reached for the wooden panel in the back of the closet. She slid it to the side to reveal the safe. Her hand trembled when she touched the combination lock. She punched in the eight-digit code, but a beep sounded, and an error sign flashed.

"Fuck!" She was shaking too much.

"Take a breath," Jay said calmly beside her.

"Twenty-five seconds left," Fox said through the cell phone.

The second time she entered the combination, she heard the click of the safe opening, turned the handle, and pulled.

She reached inside, pulled out her computer and the external hard drive, and handed it to Jay.

"Fifteen seconds to go."

Olivia slammed the safe shut, turned the handle, then spun the manual dial to lock the door. Quickly, she slid the wood panel in front of the safe and stepped out of the closet. She gripped the closet's sliding door, when it jammed. She jerked on it, but it didn't move, and she shot Jay a panicked look.

He pressed the computer and hard drive into her hands, and crouched down, pulling on a sock that had gotten stuck on the track.

"Ten seconds," Fox advised.

"Almost there," Jay said and was finally able to pull the sock out, toss it back in the closet and slide the closet door shut.

They were both racing out of the office, through the short hallway, and through the living room into the foyer. Olivia ran through the door first, Jay on her heels, pulling the door shut behind him, the key still in the lock. He turned it.

"Two seconds."

Jay pulled the key out of the lock. "We're out."

Olivia breathed hard, her chest heaving, her heart hammering up into her throat. "We did it."

Jay put his phone into his pocket and smiled at her, already ushering her to where they'd parked the car. She noticed that Jay was glancing up and down the street, always vigilant.

"Did anybody see us?" she asked, concerned.

"No, we're good. Now let's go see the others."

24

Jay and Olivia dumped the stolen car close to a Metro station in Washington D.C., and took public transportation to a station in the outskirts of D.C. where one of the other agents, Ace, picked them up with a white medical transport van.

It was early evening when they arrived at the mansion. Olivia was impressed by the beautiful villa surrounded by lush grounds. "Is this yours?", she asked Ace.

"Yes. It belonged to my father. I inherited it after Smith murdered him."

Shock charged through her. "I'm so sorry."

Ace simply gave a nod. "He ran the program at the CIA that we were all part of."

"Jay told me a little about the gift you all have. To see the future. It's fascinating."

"And the reason why Smith is after us." In the entrance hall of the large property, he ushered them toward a door on the left. "Everybody's in the kitchen."

Olivia followed him, Jay at her side, as they entered the enormous kitchen with the large dining table. Several men and women were already crowding around the table, and turned around when she entered.

"Hey, everybody," Ace said. "This is Olivia. Olivia, this is Phoebe, Michelle, Lilly, and Fox. Yankee you've already met briefly."

"Hi," she said, "It'll probably take me a little while to remember everybody's names."

Phoebe, who appeared to be heavily pregnant, addressed her, "I'll show you later where you and Jay are staying, but let's have something to eat first. Lilly helped me make dinner."

"Can I help with anything?" Olivia asked.

"No, it's ready. And the guys will clean up later," she said with a look at Ace. "Right?"

"Absolutely," Ace replied and kissed her on the cheek, before he helped her sit down at the dining table.

The dining table was already set, and everybody joined Phoebe, and helped themselves to the various dishes laid out in the center of the table. Olivia sat down next to Jay. She wasn't very hungry, since she'd had a large lunch with her parents, but she put a small amount of salad on her plate.

"Are you guys running facial recognition on Smith yet?" Jay asked.

"Yep," Fox said, "we started the moment we had a clear picture of him. It'll take a while though."

"More than just a while," Michelle added. "There are millions of pictures and video recordings, and we've gotta be thorough."

"Michelle's right," Fox added, "and we had to loosen the parameters to allow for the possibility that Smith is wearing disguises, which means we might get some false positives, which we have to check manually. Michelle and I will take the first shift after dinner. With some luck, we'll find out by tomorrow morning who he really is."

"And then?" Olivia asked. "What will you do with him once you know who he is? Will you kill him?" That thought sent a shudder down her back.

"We can't," Jay said. "Smith isn't the head of the operation. He reports to somebody. He calls him Jones. But we have no idea yet who this Jones is. We need Smith to lead us to him, so we can take down their operation in one fell swoop."

"And the CIA can't help you? There must be somebody there that—"

"We can't trust anybody. We suspect that Smith is part of the CIA, and we have no idea how high up this goes, and how many people are involved in this. They were able to kill Ace's father, the director of our program, and send over thirty precognitive agents running for their lives. They know things they shouldn't know."

Olivia cast a look at the other three agents

and realized something. "Have you considered the possibility that Smith is a precognitive too?"

"We thought of that possibility too. But when I was close to him, I didn't feel it."

Olivia stared at him. "What do you mean by *feel*?"

"Whenever a precognitive is physically close to another precognitive, we get a tingling sensation on our skin. It's like recognizing like. I didn't get that feeling from Smith."

Jay looked at his fellow agents, and they all nodded.

"Jay is correct. We all feel that tingling sensation when we're close to each other," Yankee said. "But unfortunately, the only one who was ever physically close to Smith was Tiger. And if he says he didn't feel it, then Smith isn't a precognitive."

"But it's possible that somebody who works for him, or maybe even Jones, is a precognitive," Jay said. "It's also possible that one of the agents from the program went to the dark side and is working with Smith now."

"Wouldn't be a first," Yankee threw in. "I knew one of them, Echo, who was lured to Smith's side. He's dead now."

"And all the others?" Olivia asked. "Jay, you said there were thirty agents. They can't all have allied themselves with Smith, not if they know what Smith is gonna do to them."

"No," Ace said, "but it's hard to find somebody who doesn't want to be found, particularly somebody who was trained by the CIA to be invisible."

"I still can't wrap my head around the fact that you're all former CIA agents, and that you have premonitions. What was that program at the CIA about? Or do you have to kill me if you tell me?"

Jay chuckled and winked. "Michelle, Phoebe, and Lilly all know about it, and they're still alive."

The others laughed.

"Have you ever heard of remote viewing?" Ace asked.

"Yeah, I've read about it. It's supposed to be a spying method, where the spy sits in a room and tries to psychically see something in a different place, right?"

"Pretty much," Ace said. "Back in the 90s, there was a program like that at the CIA, but it ultimately failed because the agents recruited for the program had no psychic abilities. However, my father knew that the program could be a success, if only they recruited people who had a precognitive gift. Like himself."

"So you inherited this gift from your father?" Olivia asked. "It's genetic?"

Ace shook his head. "Henry Sheppard wasn't my biological father. He adopted me when he realized that I had the gift. He started the Stargate program again in the early 2000s, and I became his first agent. Over the following years he recruited others with the same gift. But the program was top-secret, and not even the top brass at the agency knew about it."

"But how's that possible? I mean, somebody must have paid for the program." Nothing was for free.

"He managed to divert money from other programs to finance Stargate," Ace explained. "After all, most budgets at government agencies are so inflated that nobody notices when a few million dollars go missing."

"Your tax dollars hard at work," Jay added.

"I'll keep that in mind next time I send the IRS my hard-earned money," Olivia said, smirking.

"Speaking of hard-earned money," Michelle interjected. "Can I just say that I love your books? *Galaxy Outcast* is amazing."

Olivia froze. They knew that she was T.R. Harland? She caught Jay's apologetic gaze.

"Don't blame Jay," Fox said quickly. "But when he thought you were planning to kill him, we had to dig into your background, and confirm that you're not a psychotic killer."

Stunned, Olivia's chin dropped. She stared at Jay. "You thought I was planning to kill you? Why?"

Jay grimaced. "Remember that I told you I bugged your house? The guys heard you discuss with somebody on the phone that you were trying to *off* him, but that you hadn't figured out how."

"And apparently Belladonna was getting old, and daggers made a mess," Fox tossed in with a chuckle.

It dawned on her then. "Oh my God, I was discussing the plot for my next book with my sister."

"Yeah, we figured that out later," Jay said, "after you tossed me out on my ass that night."

She shook her head, everything about that night coming back to her now. "You seemed so different that night." Yet he'd made love to her nevertheless. But had that been his intent, or had he come to do something entirely different? "Did you come to kill me that night?"

Jay immediately took her hand. "No, baby, I didn't. I tried to figure out why you were planning to kill me, so I could change your mind." He put his hand on her cheek and drew closer. "I could never hurt you."

She saw the truth in his eyes and kissed him. Their lips fused, and Jay put his arms around her and held her tightly.

"Get a room," Yankee said.

Jay released her, not looking embarrassed at all, and cast Yankee a sideways look. "Not a bad idea."

25

By the next morning, the search with the facial recognition software had yielded no actionable results. While Smith had shown up on various traffic cams as well as security cameras all over Washington D.C., none had given any indication as to who he was, where he was going, and where he came from. None of them had been with cars that would have allowed Jay and his fellow agents to trace ownership of the car, and thus reveal Smith's identity.

"I also ran his picture against all driver's licenses issued in D.C., Maryland, and Virginia. Nothing," Fox reported, swiveling away from his monitor and facing Jay and the rest of the gang.

"We know he has a driver's license," Jay said. "Maybe it was issued in another state."

Fox shrugged. "He would have had to exchange it for one in whichever state he lives now. And we're assuming he lives in D.C., Maryland, or Virginia. Everything else would be too far to drive into D.C. daily."

"Do you even know if he works in D.C.?" Olivia asked.

"If he's part of the CIA, or another government agency, which he kind of has to, given all we know about him, then he would have to live somewhere close. Which means he would have had to get a license from one of those three DMVs within sixty days of moving here," Jay explained.

"Yeah, if he changed his residence. But what if he didn't? What if he kept his official residence wherever he's from originally?" Olivia asked. "I mean, congresspeople do it all the time. They are residents of their home states, but they are in D.C. most of the year to represent their state. Smith could do the same, you know, maybe for tax reasons?"

"That's a good point," Jay admitted. He hadn't thought of that himself. He looked at Fox. "Can we run his photo through all the other DMVs in the country?"

"Sure we can," Fox said, then grimaced, "but that means hacking into every state's DMV database. That's time consuming. We need to narrow down the search."

"Let's figure out how," Ace said. "Suggestions?"

"Did Smith have an accent?" Phoebe asked. "Michelle? You spoke to him several times. And Jay too."

Jay exchanged a look with Michelle, but they both shrugged. "I couldn't hear anything in particular, but then most of the time I was drugged out of my mind after he'd captured me."

"Frankly, he sounded like he was from around here," Michelle said. "Definitely not a Southerner, nor from New York. Those accents I'd recognize."

Yankee nodded. "When he had Lilly in his

grips at that warehouse we blew up, I was too focused on trying to free Lilly that I wasn't paying attention."

"He didn't say much anyway," Lilly confirmed, "but I'm with Michelle. He's not a Southerner or a New Yorker."

"Then maybe we should do what I suggested to Jay yesterday," Olivia said. "Go through the guest list of my sister's wedding, and eliminate everybody we can identify via social media and driver's licenses and whatever else Fox and Michelle can find on the internet. Whoever we can't identify must be Smith."

Jay exchanged a look with the other three Stargate agents. "Worth a shot. The list can't be that long. Right, Olivia? Maybe two hundred people?"

"More like three hundred, but we can exclude the women immediately. That brings it down to less than a hundred-and-fifty. And I'll recognize at least a few of the guests."

"Let's do it," Ace agreed.

"Okay, I'll get my computer," Olivia said.

Minutes later, Olivia sat at a desk in the

computer room, her laptop in front of her, Fox by her side.

"Here's the spreadsheet," she explained. "In the first column are the people who got invited; their addresses are in column two. The third column shows who confirmed that they were coming. And in the fourth column are any additional notes such as somebody requesting a vegan meal or reporting any food allergies."

"Wow, you'd never know you were the creative type," Fox said.

"Writers have to be organized," Olivia replied.

"Okay," Fox said, speaking to everybody now. "We'll all take names from the list and start digging in."

Jay put his hand on Olivia's shoulder, and she looked up at him. "Olivia, you'll need to take those people off that you know can't be Smith, starting with your family, the bridesmaids, the groom and so on."

She nodded. "I'm on it." She started highlighting names and making notes next to them and looked up at the gang. "There were a few of Timothy's college buddies I danced with. Those I'll exclude too. They're too young to be Smith. And I took a photo of the groom's father, and Jay didn't recognize him as Smith either. Then there are the women, those can go too." She tapped on her keyboard and continued highlighting.

"Here we go."

"Let me project the list on the large screen on the wall," Fox said and reached for a cable, and plugged it into one of the ports on Olivia's laptop.

An instant later, the list filled the monitor on the wall.

"Okay," Jay said, "Ace, take line one, Yankee three, Phoebe seven, Lilly ten, Olivia eleven, I'll take thirteen. Start with social media accounts: Facebook, Instagram, Twitter, whatever you can find. And if you can't find any information on your target, hand the name over to Michelle or Fox, and they'll hack the appropriate DMVs to get the driver's licenses."

They got to work. Some people were easier to find and eliminate, mostly the younger ones. They had Instagram accounts and tweeted, and even posted pictures of the wedding on their social media accounts, making it even easier to eliminate them. The older men were a little harder to find. Only a few had Facebook accounts, and very few posted photos, though some of them could be eliminated by their wives' social media accounts. The men with rather common first and last names were the hardest to identify, guests like Mark Jennings for example. There were dozens of Facebook accounts under that name. Even narrowing down the hits by location didn't help much, since many Facebook users didn't disclose where they lived. Those were the names Fox and Michelle spent their time on getting information via the DMV or other governmental agencies.

Within five hours, they'd whittled down the list to a handful of names.

Jay exchanged a concerned look with Ace. "It's not looking good."

Two more names were crossed off the list, and Olivia looked at them, just as disappointed, while Fox and Michelle were working on the last two remaining names.

They too turned away from their computers a minute later and shook their heads.

"Those two are clear too," Michelle said. "Sorry."

"How can that be?" Jay said, rubbing his nape. "He was clearly at the wedding. He wasn't a waiter, and he was around when the group photo was taken, but was smart enough to turn away."

"Do you think he crashed the wedding?" Yankee asked.

"To what purpose?" Jay shook his head. "No, he must have been invited."

"Then why didn't he show up on the list?" Ace asked. "He must have come with somebody, right?"

Olivia suddenly gasped. "That's it. He came with somebody who was invited. He was a *plus one*." She started to tap on her keyboard and sorted the list in a different way. "There." She pointed to the screen. "Three guests, all women, accepted the invitation and confirmed that they were bringing a date, but they didn't give their date's name. Smith must be one of these dates."

"Brilliant!" Jay said and pressed a kiss to Olivia's cheek. "Do you recognize any of the names, Olivia?"

She looked at the list again. "Yes, Evelyn Treadstone is Timothy's mother. She's divorced from Timothy's father, and she hasn't remarried. She's using her maiden name again. And this one, Mercedes Bosch, I remember her name because it was so unusual, you know, two German brand names. She's some relative from the Midwest, she's in her fifties or sixties for sure, and she brought a young guy. He looked like a gigolo. I remember because my sister made a comment that she was the black sheep of Timothy's family."

"And the third woman?" Jay asked.

"Jane Karlinski? No idea, sorry."

"Okay," Fox said, "I'll take her. Michelle, take Timothy's mother and find out who she's dating."

They all watched Fox and Michelle do what they did best, scour the internet for information, and hack into government servers.

Fox was the first to report what he'd found.

"Jane Karlinski was accompanied by William Karlinski, her seventy-year-old father. He's not Smith."

Jay sighed, holding out hope that Michelle would have better luck.

"You guys are staring holes into my back," Michelle said without looking over her shoulder.

It took a few more minutes, during which nobody spoke, until Michelle finally turned around.

"May I present, Evelyn Treadstone's date. She only refers to him as John."

Jay stared at the monitor. Michelle had found a snapshot of Evelyn Treadstone dancing with Smith.

"So you think his name is actually John Smith? There must be thousands of men named John Smith," Olivia said in disbelief.

"It's not his real name," Michelle said. "When I met him in that parking garage where he gave me instructions to hunt the person hacking into the CIA's servers, I asked him who he was. And he said, and I quote *how about Smith?* His first name may well be John.

But since his date doesn't mention his last name anywhere, nor does she tag him in her post, we can't be sure of his real name."

"So we're at a dead end?" Olivia asked.

"No," Jay answered immediately. "If he's dating Timothy's mother, we can put surveillance on her. Eventually she'll meet up with him, and then we can follow him and see where he leads us."

Ace nodded. "Let's tap her phone, and set up a camera outside her home to record him and his car if he's showing up there. Fox?"

"No problem. I'll get the phone surveillance started."

"Yankee and I can install the camera tonight," Jay said.

"Okay, we've got a plan," Ace said. "Let's get that bastard."

26

After dinner the same day, Jay and Yankee readied their equipment to install surveillance outside the house of Evelyn Treadstone. They were busy disguising the van as one from DC Gas & Electric, so nobody seeing them would become suspicious.

"We've never gotten this close to identifying him," Yankee said.

"I wish we could kill him right now." But Jay knew that was impossible.

"Me too, especially because he tried to have Lilly killed. Twice! But he has to lead us to Jones first. But when it's time to take him out, I'm calling dibs," Yankee vowed.

"Knowing what I know about Ace so far, he's gonna wanna take him out himself."

"Yeah, well, he'll have to get in line."

Jay chuckled and put a large decal on the door of the white van. "I don't care who kills him, as long as he's dead."

"So, you and Olivia," Yankee said, changing the subject. "How's that going?"

"It's going well. She's a very forgiving person. Not sure if a different woman would have forgiven me so quickly for bugging her place."

"Doesn't surprise me that she forgave you. I mean, the way she looks at you..." Yankee shook his head. "Lucky bastard."

Jay grinned. He knew he'd struck gold with Olivia, even though she hadn't yet spoken the three words he wanted to hear from her. But he could be patient.

"Looks like we're ready," Yankee said with a look at the van. "Now let's get into some overalls so we'll look the part."

They walked back into the house, when Ace

came toward them and waved them into the computer room. "Surveillance is off."

"Why?" Jay asked, surprised as he and Yankee entered the room.

"We just intercepted a call between Evelyn Treadstone and Smith. Michelle confirmed that it was his voice. Smith and Timothy's mother got into an argument, and she broke it off. She was pissed off that he made her leave her son's wedding reception early, and blames him for getting into a fight with her son because of it. And then Smith didn't even stay the night with her. She accused him of two-timing her. So, unless they reconcile, which I wouldn't hold my breath for, we won't be able to identify him by surveilling Evelyn Treadstone."

"Fuck!" Jay cursed. "Now we're back to square one."

Olivia stood up from where she'd been sitting with her computer. "Maybe not."

He watched her walk closer. "What do you mean?"

"Remember when you listened to me talking to my sister on the phone and thought I was planning to kill you?" she asked.

"Yeah, but what's that got to do with Smith?"

Fox and Michelle also came closer to listen to what Olivia was suggesting.

"It gave me an idea. Smith bugged my place, which means he can listen in on me now. And he has no idea that we know that he's recording everything that happens in my house. We can set a trap."

Slowly, it dawned on Jay. He realized what Olivia was suggesting. "That's too dangerous."

"It's not," she protested. "He has no idea that we know that he somehow connected me to you. We can exploit that, and stage something for him. It's easy. And then we control the where and when. We'll be in the driver's seat."

Jay didn't like the idea.

"She's smart," Ace said with a sideways look at Jay. "And it would definitely give us the advantage. It'll be easy to keep an eye on Olivia."

"What if something goes wrong?" Jay asked.

"It won't." Ace motioned to the other

agents and their girlfriends. "We outnumber him. And with the right disguises, he won't spot us, and we can tail him until he leads us to his car, his home, or his office. It's our chance to identify him."

Jay looked at Olivia and held her determined gaze. "Fine. We'll do it. First thing tomorrow morning."

Just before Olivia entered her cottage, she switched her cell phone back on. It was a precautionary measure in case Smith was tracking her phone. She hadn't switched it on since Jay had stolen the car after the lunch with her parents.

The leather travel bag she'd used during her short stay at the wedding hotel in her hand, she entered her home and did what she normally did when she got home. Jay had told her to act as normal as possible. Olivia tossed her bag on the floor, then picked up the mail that had collected on the floor of the foyer. She tossed most of it straight in the trash—

solicitations, and flyers from a local supermarket.

She went to the fridge, pulled out a bottle of water and took a large gulp, not bothering with a glass.

When her cell phone rang, she knew who it was before she even looked at the display. She pulled it from her handbag, then clicked on answer.

"Oh, hey, Jay!" she said cheerfully, then put him on speaker, while she put the bottle of water back in the fridge and opened a cupboard. She snatched a package of cookies and looked for a pair of scissors to open it.

"Where were you? I was trying to call you all day yesterday," Jay asked.

"I told you my parents were still here. So I stayed with them in D.C. for an extra day."

"You could at least have answered my calls."

"Sorry, but my battery died. I mean, totally died. I had to find a store to get the right replacement battery." This statement would give Smith an explanation why her cell phone was off for nearly two days.

"I'm relieved. When I couldn't get a hold of you... well, anyway. Just wanted to say hi."

"It's good to hear your voice. I was thinking, you know I have nothing in the fridge, and I have to go back into D.C., because I forgot to pick up the book I'd ordered from the specialty bookstore near Dupont Circle, so how about lunch in the city?"

"Uhm, yeah, I'm not sure... I'm kind of busy," Jay said.

"Oh come on, just an hour. You can't be all that busy. There's this French place on 14th Street. It's called Le Diplomate, and they have an outdoor terrace. Why don't you meet me there, let's say at noon?"

"Well, okay, I guess I have to eat anyway."

"Great! Can't wait to see you. And please, don't be late like last time. I hate waiting. Especially in a restaurant. It's so embarrassing." She pouted.

"I'll be there."

"Bye." Olivia disconnected the call, and went into her bedroom to get changed.

27

Jay had chosen the Le Diplomate restaurant on 14th Street in the Cardozo neighborhood of Washington D.C. because it was a busy area during lunch and dinner time, with several restaurants with outdoor seating at each block of the six-block commercial stretch. There were only two Metro stations within a comfortable walking distance, Dupont Circle and U-Shaw Howard. However, it was possible that Smith would show up by car, if he felt reasonably comfortable that he could get street parking.

Jay was prepared for everything. Wearing a

fat suit to make himself look like a heavy-set man in his sixties, with grey hair, bushy grey eyebrows, and a stubble beard, and dressed in baggy pants and a casual long-sleeved shirt, he sat in a red sedan with an Uber sticker in the window.

Yankee was disguised as well, and not even Jay would have recognized him. He had long dark-brown hair, John Lennon glasses, and looked like an absent-minded professor. He sat at one of the outside tables, a full plate of food in front of him, while reading a book. His moped was parked on the same block.

Ace and Phoebe were also disguised, though Phoebe's pregnant belly showed prominently. They were making good use of this feature, and carried a few bags from local boutiques, and continued to browse in the stores along the street.

Fox looked like the quintessential tourist, a selfie-stick in his hand, a guidebook sticking out of his jacket pocket, sunglasses and a baseball cap on his head. He wore shorts, a Washington D.C. T-shirt and sneakers.

Even Lilly was in on the surveillance. She

wore a business suit and looked like a successful woman working in an office, her ear glued to the phone. She too wore a wig and dark glasses, so Smith wouldn't be able to recognize her.

Michelle was back at the villa, coordinating the cameras and communication devices everybody was wearing hidden on their clothing. The earpieces they wore were either cleverly hidden by long hair like in Yankee's, Lilly's, and Phoebe's case, or covered by modeling dough matching their respective skin color.

They'd all arrived an hour before the lunch date Olivia had arranged with Jay, knowing that Smith would try to arrive before Olivia to stake out the place and figure out the best position from where to watch for Jay's arrival. Jay assumed that Smith too would arrive in some sort of disguise, though he couldn't imagine that his disguise would be as elaborate as Jay's and his friends'.

Olivia arrived at the restaurant a few minutes before noon, and got a table on the terrace facing the street, close to where

Yankee was sitting. Yankee was asking the waitress for the check, because he needed to be prepared to leave at a moment's notice, and didn't want to run off without paying.

Jay communicated with the others via his earpiece. Olivia was the only one who didn't wear one. The risk that Smith might detect surveillance equipment on her was too great.

"Any sightings yet?" Jay asked, speaking quietly into his microphone.

"Negative," Ace replied.

He received the same reply from all of the others, except for Fox.

"I have a possible. The guy in the suit and the sunglasses looking at the newspaper rack just outside the convenience store."

Jay adjusted his rearview mirror so it captured the sidewalk just outside the convenience store which lay behind him. There was indeed a man perusing the newspapers and magazines. He took one, went into the store, presumably to pay, and then emerged a moment later. Instead of walking away, he hung around there, pretending to read, while his gaze drifted across the street to the restaurant where Olivia sat in plain view.

Despite the sunglasses, Jay recognized him. "It's him. You all know what to do. Michelle, the clock is running."

"Understood," Michelle said through the earpiece.

For the next fifteen minutes, Ace and Phoebe went from boutique to boutique, while Fox perused the menus of various different restaurants as if looking for the best deal, while Lilly ordered an espresso from a coffeeshop and sat down on a chair outside it, and scribbled in her datebook as if making important business notes. Jay continued sitting in the car pretending to wait for his next fare, and Yankee paid his check at the restaurant, but he hadn't finished his drink yet, so he remained sitting there.

While the clock ticked away, Olivia looked at her watch several times, and when the waitress asked her if she wanted to order something, she ordered a soda and told her she was waiting for a friend, and would order when her friend arrived. Meanwhile, Smith moved around too. He walked to Etto's, the restaurant closest to Olivia's and looked at the menu posted outside, while glancing toward Olivia. When a hostess asked him if he wanted a table, he declined, saying he wasn't ready to eat.

After twenty minutes, Michelle announced through the communications system, "Ready for playback?"

"It's a go," Jay said.

A moment later, he heard the ringing of a phone in his ear, and saw that Olivia picked up her cell phone and answered the call with a sigh.

"Where are you?" Olivia asked impatiently.

Then the recording he'd prepared earlier started playing, and he heard his own voice through the earpiece.

"I'm sorry, baby, something came up."

"What do you mean something came up? I've been waiting here for almost half an hour."

"I just can't make it today. There's too much going on. Sorry. I'll make it up to you."

"This is the third time now that you stood me up. You know what, Jay? Don't bother!

You're just not worth the hassle. Don't call me anymore."

"But Olivia—"

Olivia disconnected the call, and put the phone on the table, annoyed. Jay was proud of her. She'd learned her lines, and she'd delivered them with perfect timing. While he didn't think that Smith could hear every word of her conversation from where he stood, it was possible that he'd bugged her phone, therefore the recording of Jay's side of the conversation had been necessary.

While Olivia paid for her drink and then rose to make her way back to the Metro station, Smith turned away in the other direction.

"He's on the move," Jay confirmed.

Jay waited patiently as Smith walked past his car, then turned on the engine, but he didn't pull out of his parking spot immediately.

"Ace, he's turning onto Corcoran Street."

"Got him," Ace replied. "He's getting into a beat-up Ford Taurus, color white." Then Ace recited the license plate number.

"Which state?" Michelle asked immediately.

"West Virginia."

"On it," Michelle confirmed.

"He's in the car," Ace announced.

"I can see him," Yankee said, now on his moped. "He's turning on 13th Street toward Logan Circle."

"I'll head him off at Logan Circle," Jay said and started driving.

At the corner, Jay picked up Ace and Phoebe, who got in the back of the car as if they were paying passengers. Yankee was following Smith with his moped, while Fox confirmed that he was getting into a white van with Lilly.

As they followed Smith through the city, they handed off surveillance to each other in regular intervals, the same vehicle never following him more than two or three blocks on the quiet streets, or five or six blocks on the busier ones, just like they'd been taught at The Farm. With three different vehicles following Smith—one van, one fake Uber sedan, and one moped—Jay was confident that their target wouldn't catch onto them.

"I got a name off the license plate," Michelle suddenly said through the communication system. "Car's registered to a Katherine Snell, lives in Inwood, West Virginia. But according to the woman's driver's license, she's eighty-four years old and doesn't drive anymore. I think the car might be stolen. Sorry."

"Crap!" Jay hissed.

"Not so fast," Fox said through the earpiece. "Baby, can you check whether she has relatives? Sons, nephews, grandsons? Maybe she gave the car to one of them?"

"I'll check that," Michelle replied.

"There," Ace now said. "He's heading into the underground garage of that condo building on the corner."

Jay simply drove past it. "Fox, Lilly, you're up."

"We got it," Fox replied.

Jay gave Michelle the address. "Michelle, looks like there are six or eight condos in that building. Get a list of the owners." He stopped the car a block away on a side street.

"I'm on it," Michelle replied.

"Cruising by," Fox said. "Taking a turn around the block. Yankee?"

"I'm two blocks back," Yankee confirmed. "I've got the garage door in my line of sight. I'm stopped at the curb. Stay out of sight for now."

A few minutes passed without anything happening, until Yankee suddenly said, "Garage door is opening again. A black SUV is coming out, heading my way."

"I'll catch him two blocks farther down," Fox said. "Did you get a license plate?"

"Negative," Yankee said. "No license plate on the front of the car. But it's definitely Smith driving."

Jay made a U-turn on a side street and headed back the way he'd come, following in the direction the SUV had left. Before he reached the SUV, he saw Fox's van.

"Michelle, I've got the license plate," Fox said and recited the number. "It's a Virginia license plate."

"Got it," Michelle confirmed.

"Jay, take over for me," Fox said and put his turn signal on to turn off onto a side street.

"I'm on him," Jay said.

As traffic became busier, Jay kept the others apprised of the SUV's movements, staying far enough away so Smith wouldn't become suspicious, and every so often changing positions with Fox, and Yankee.

"He's heading for the freeway," Fox said.

"That leaves me in the dust," Yankee said. "Signing off, heading back to the mansion."

"Roger that, Yankee," Ace said.

After several minutes on the freeway heading west, Ace added, "Michelle, anything on that license plate?"

"Yep, which is to say it's a blocked number. So he's either law enforcement or—"

"CIA," Jay said and pointed to the freeway signs indicating where they were heading. "He's going to Langley."

"So our suspicions were right all along. Smith works for the CIA."

"That would explain the blocked license plate," Fox said.

"So we're at a dead end?" Phoebe asked.

"No," Michelle interrupted. "I've got the list of the condo owners. One name sticks out. Katherine Snell, the old woman who owns the Ford Taurus."

"Okay, let's dig into her," Jay said. "Smith must be connected to her somehow."

"I'll start digging."

When Smith took the exit for Langley, Jay and Fox followed. Minutes later it was clear that he was indeed heading toward the CIA's headquarters in Langley. When Jay saw Smith's SUV turn down the road that led to the CIA campus, he drove past it.

"Let's meet at home," Jay decided. "This is as far as we can take it today."

By the time they all arrived back at Ace's mansion, Yankee was already expecting them. "Michelle has news." He ushered them into the computer room. The wall monitor showed a driver's license with Smith's picture.

"Meet John Bancroft. His driver's license is from West Virginia, which is why we didn't get any hits when we only looked at D.C., Maryland, and Virginia earlier."

"Yes!" Jay called out excitedly. "We've got the bastard."

"That's not all," Michelle said with a grin. "He's the nephew of Katherine Snell in whose name the Ford Taurus is registered, and who's on the deed for the condo in D.C. But I'm pretty sure the old lady doesn't live there. The home address the Ford Taurus is registered to is in Inwood, WV, and judging by the utility bills of the house she lives in, she still lives in West Virginia. Her nephew is probably using her name as cover for his safe house, because that condo isn't the only property connected to him."

Fox grinned and put his arm over Michelle's shoulder. "Look at my hacker girl." He kissed her on the cheek.

"Even though the address on Smith's license is his aunt's house in Inwood, I found a house owned by a John Bancroft in Fort Washington, Maryland. It's overlooking the Potomac." She looked at Fox, then pulled up a Google image of the address she'd found. "Look familiar?"

"Oh my God," Fox said and pointed to the

large house with the enormous wooden deck facing the river. Several boats could be seen on the water. "That's it."

"What is it?" Jay asked, confused.

Fox looked at him. "That's the house from my premonition, the house I'm at when the explosion happens. I'm at Smith's house. He's the one giving me the drink that paralyzes me, so I can't do anything to prevent the disaster."

Ace patted Fox on the shoulder. "We're close now. We can stop Smith, just as soon as he leads us to Jones."

Jay nodded, exchanging encouraging looks with his fellow agents. "That bastard's days are numbered."

Ace grinned back at him. "Soon, there'll be justice."

"To justice," Jay said, and the other's repeated the words.

"To justice."

28

Olivia was back at her cottage, spending the entire afternoon with the TV on for background noise. She was still performing for Smith, playing the annoyed girlfriend who'd finally had enough of the man who had stood her up once too often. On her way home, she'd left a message for her sister, because she needed Grace to finalize the last part of her plan to deceive Smith.

When her sister finally called in the early evening, Olivia took a deep breath, answered the call and put her on the speaker. "Hey, sis. How's the honeymoon?"

"Fabulous. But how are you? Mom said you met a guy." Grace chuckled. "Well, she actually said you were trying to hide him in your hotel room. Girl! Why didn't you tell me you were seeing somebody?"

She'd counted on her mother telling Grace the latest gossip, and on the fact that Grace would immediately steer the conversation in that direction.

"Well, I wish Mom hadn't said anything."

"Why not? She said he's handsome."

"Yeah, he is. But he's also totally unreliable. That's why I didn't mention him before."

Grace sighed. "Most men are a little unreliable."

"I know that, but Jay is worse than any of the guys I've dated before. I mean, the sex is great, don't get me wrong. But he's always so secretive, and we make plans, and then he just doesn't show, and calls me way later to tell me he got delayed. Total bullshit."

"Oh, I'm sorry, Liv. Mom thought you'd finally found a nice guy."

Olivia sighed heavily. "Yeah, so did I. But when he already starts out like that at the beginning and lies to me and makes excuses, it'll just get worse later. You know? I don't need that kind of trouble in my life. So I told him it's over."

"So sorry. I wish I were there and we could go out for a drink. Are you gonna be all right?"

She shrugged. "I will be. I'm sure. But I need a change of scenery."

"A little vacation? You deserve it. You've been working so hard."

"Yeah, a bit more than just a vacation. You know when we talked a few months ago about one day going to Japan to see where Dad's grandparents are from?"

"I wish we could have done that trip together, but Timothy—"

"No, no, I know that. You're a couple now. You can't just go off on some trip with me. But I figured, what am I waiting for? I can do my job from anywhere in the world. So why not from Japan? I might as well immerse myself in the culture and all, and brush up on my Japanese."

"Are you sure? Why don't you talk to Mom and Dad and see if they wanna go with you?"

"I wanna go on an adventure for once in my life, you know? So I checked the flights today, and there are a few last-minute flights that are dirt-cheap. So I booked one. For tomorrow."

"Tomorrow? Are you crazy?"

"You're always telling me I'm not spontaneous enough. Now I'm spontaneous."

"Are you sure you're not just doing this because it didn't work out with this guy?"

Olivia shrugged. "So what if? It doesn't change anything about the fact that I've always wanted to go to Japan. And who knows, maybe I'll find myself a nice Japanese man."

Grace laughed. "Have you told Mom and Dad yet?"

"I'll call them from Tokyo. Or they'll just try to talk me out of it. And before I forget it, my cell phone won't work in Japan. I'll get a new SIM card when I arrive. So don't worry if you can't reach me by phone immediately. If there's anything urgent, just email me."

"Looks like your mind is made up. And I know better than to talk you out of it. That's never worked before. So, promise me something, little sis: be careful, send me lots of updates, and most of all, have fun."

"I will. I love you, Grace."

"I love you too."

"Tell that husband of yours to treat you well." Tears were now welling up in her eyes, because this would truly be good-bye until it was safe to come back to her old life.

"I will," Grace said.

Olivia ended the call and sniffled, wiping her tears.

Then she walked into her bedroom and started packing everything that she would need for the next few months. Leaving her cottage and not being able to see her family would be bittersweet. But the ruse was necessary so Smith wouldn't realize that Jay and the other ex-CIA agents were onto him.

It was early morning, when Olivia got up and got ready to leave. She hadn't slept well, even though she knew that Jay wasn't far away and was watching her, ready to interfere, should Smith show his face unexpectedly.

An Uber took her to Dulles International Airport. The car dropped her at the departures level, and the driver lifted her two suitcases out of the trunk.

"Have a good flight," he said.

"Thank you." She took her suitcases and rolled them into the departure hall where the check-in counters for Japanese Airlines were busy processing passengers. She walked past the ticket counters and headed toward the escalators, following the signs for arrivals.

On the arrivals level of the airport, she rolled her suitcases toward the sign for ground transportation and walked through the first double doors leading outside. There, arriving passengers were waiting in line for taxis, airport and hotel shuttles, or waited for friends or an Uber to pick them up.

Olivia paved her way through the throng of passengers from an arriving flight, and steered toward the farthest end of the pick-up zone. There, she stopped. She'd memorized the license plate of the car that would pick her up.

Perspiration was now collecting on her nape, both from the early morning muggy heat, as well as her nervousness.

An unassuming silver sedan stopped, and Olivia looked at the license plate. It matched the plate she'd memorized. The driver's door opened, and a tall black man exited, and walked around the car. She looked him up and down. He was as tall as Jay, but he was heavy-set, at least eighty pounds heavier, and had grey hair and a round face.

"Ma'am?" he greeted her, and reached for her suitcases.

"Thank you," she said with a smile, and watched him as he lifted her two suitcases into the trunk.

When he closed it, Olivia got into the backseat of the car, and placed her handbag and her computer bag on the bench next to her.

Moments later, the driver got back into the car, and they drove off.

"Time to switch off your cell phone," he said with a deep Southern accent.

She powered down her phone. If Smith

tracked it, he would think that she was getting on the plane. "Thanks for the reminder, sir."

"Sir?" he asked with a chuckle. "So you're not calling me by my name anymore? I guess next time I make love to you, I should ask you to call me sir." Then he added, now in a different voice, "That might be fun."

"Jay!"

"Hey, baby."

"I didn't recognize you at all." He'd transformed himself totally.

"That was the point. Not that I think that Smith is having you followed. But Ace is keeping an eye on him nevertheless."

She let out a sigh of relief. "I missed you last night."

"I missed you too. But it was necessary." He met her eyes in the rearview mirror. "We'll make up for it tonight."

The promise she read in his eyes made up for all the anxiety she'd experienced in the past two days.

After half an hour, Jay drove into a parking structure, where Yankee, disguised as a hospital orderly, was waiting for them with a white van with decals on its sides that indicated that this was a medical transport vehicle.

Yankee transferred her luggage to the white van, while Jay wiped down the interior and the doors of the silver sedan for fingerprints, before removing the license plates and taking them with him. Beneath the license plates were different ones that actually belonged to the car.

"Let's go," Yankee ordered, and Olivia sat in the back of the van with Jay, while Yankee drove.

Jay put his arms around Olivia and kissed her. "All went well. Smith has no idea that we played him. We know who he is now. And he does work for the CIA, just like we suspected."

"I'm glad it worked. But what if Smith realizes that I never flew to Japan? Won't he then suspect that this was just a ruse?"

"He won't realize that you never arrived in Tokyo. Fox has everything in place to hack into the airline's records to show that you boarded your flight and landed safely. He'll even falsify the records of the Japanese authorities to show that you went through immigration and customs. Don't worry. He's good. For all intents and purposes you're not living in the US anymore. And Smith has no reason to think otherwise."

"That'll piss him off," Yankee said from the driver's seat.

Olivia chuckled. "You guys are so good at what you do."

Jay waggled his grey eyebrows. "Well, we *are* secret agents, you know, comes with the territory."

Then he silenced her giggles with a kiss, and she didn't object.

29

Jay pulled the door to his room in Ace's villa shut behind him. They'd tied up loose ends, making sure Smith—or rather, John Bancroft—had no idea that they were onto him. But they'd also celebrated. For the first time in many years, there was hope that they would be able to stop their enemies and make sure the doomsday premonition they were all seeing in their dreams would never come to pass.

Jay got undressed in the dark, not wanting to wake Olivia. Naked, he slipped beneath the covers, when he felt Olivia stir.

"Jay?" she murmured and turned.

He reached for her and realized that she was naked too. Unable to resist, he pulled her into his arms. "I didn't mean to wake you."

She ran her hands over his torso and reached between his legs, touching his cock. She stroked him gently, and he already felt blood rushing to it. They lay on their sides, facing each other.

"I should let you sleep," he murmured, before he captured her lips, kissing her tenderly. Olivia responded with a soft moan, and her hand on his cock stilled, but the damage was already done: he was hard, and he wouldn't get any sleep, until he'd stilled the need Olivia had awoken in him.

He caressed her breasts, kneading them in his palms, squeezing the supple flesh, and eliciting soft sighs from its owner, while he shoved one thigh between her legs and rubbed against her pussy. Warm dew rained on his skin, showing him that Olivia was ready for him.

He severed the kiss. "Tell me, are there times when you're not horny?"

She rubbed herself against his thigh.

"When I'm with you, I can't think of anything else but having you inside me."

"And why is that?" he coaxed. He removed his leg from between hers and brought his hand to her moist cleft, rubbing over her warm flesh.

Olivia sighed contentedly. "You make me feel like nobody else before."

He stroked his finger upward, until he found her clit.

A moan burst from her lips. "Oh, just like that." She lifted her lashes to look into his eyes. "The other night you said you had no right to ask me to be with you. But that was before we knew that Smith had already connected me to you. So I was wondering, would you ask me now to be with you? Since now we're both on the run."

"And what would you say if I asked you now?"

"I'd have to say what I wanted to say the other night."

"Which is?"

"That I love you."

His heart felt as if it was bursting. "Olivia, I

can't tell you how happy you make me by saying that." He kissed her passionately. "I love you."

She smiled at him. "Then why don't you show me how much?" She put her hand on his rock-hard cock and squeezed him.

"Tell me how you want it." Because as long as he could sink his aching cock into her soft pussy, he didn't care how.

"I loved it how you took me in the foyer against the wall. It was so raw, so primal."

He remembered exactly why it had felt that way. "That's when I believed you were plotting to kill me. I tried to make you see that I'm more use to you alive than dead."

"I liked that. I like feeling how strong you are, and that I can't escape you."

"Fuck, baby, not another word, or I'm gonna spill before I'm even inside you." Because what she made him picture with her words turned him on like nothing before.

He tossed the sheets back and got out of bed, then helped Olivia up. He kissed her hard, then turned her against the wall next to the bed.

"Brace your hands against the wall," he ordered.

He watched her as she followed his instruction then spread her legs, her beautiful ass pointed at him.

"Like that?" she asked like an innocent.

He palmed both cheeks and dropped his face to her neck. "You know exactly how."

Jay bent his knees and adjusted his cock. When its tip touched the entrance to Olivia's body, he took a deep breath, before thrusting forward and plunging deep and hard into her pussy. Warmth and wetness wrapped around him like silk. He had to catch his breath, the feeling of being imprisoned in her sheath so intense that it threatened to overwhelm him.

"You're the sexiest woman I've ever met," he murmured into her ear, while thrusting in and out of her tight channel. He loved the feeling of skin on skin as their bodies moved in sync. The sounds of their breaths and their moans filled the room, but Jay didn't care if anybody heard them or not. One day, they would live within their own four walls, but until then, this would have to do.

"I love you, Olivia."

"I love you, Jay."

"Now be a good girl, and come," he encouraged her and slid his right hand to her front to caress her clitoris. Olivia gasped when he rubbed his fingers over it and began to draw small circles around it. By now, he knew her body so well. He knew what aroused her most, and how he could bring her to let herself go. Giving her pleasure and deriving the same pleasure for himself was the most natural thing he'd ever done. Making love to Olivia made him feel whole again, and helped him push back the memories of his ordeal at Smith's hand. Soon, all of this would be in the past, because he could already see the future, see the life they would have.

The small house overlooked a quiet cove, and blue waves lapped at the sandy beach. Surfers rode the waves, and palm trees provided shade in the tropical garden only steps from the water's edge. He recognized his surroundings, though he'd never been to Hawaii. But he'd seen many pictures and recognized Diamond Head, the dormant volcano of Oahu, in the distance. It was a world away from Washington D.C.

When he turned around to a sound from behind him, he knew this was his home, because the woman coming out through the French doors carrying tropical drinks was Olivia. She was dressed in a traditional Hawaiian flower dress, her feet bare, her belly round and beautiful. Behind her, a little girl not older than two years followed, her skin a shade lighter than Jay's, her face as beautiful as that of her mother.

The vision blurred, and he was back in the bedroom in Ace's house making love to Olivia. Her pussy spasmed around his cock, and he felt the approach of his own orgasm. He let go of his control, and reveled in the knowledge that they would have a future together. A happy one.

Jay lifted Olivia back onto the bed, pulling her on top of him. They were both breathing hard.

"You know, there's something I don't quite understand," Olivia said.

"What is it?"

"The premonition you had about Smith."

"What about it?"

"Well, you had the premonition before you and I ever got involved, before we ran into each other at the grocery store. But we know now that the reason Smith was in my house was because he must have seen us at the hotel where the wedding took place. So if you and I had never slept with each other, he would have never seen the two of us together."

"I see where you're going. Had I not been with you, Smith would never have planted bugs in your cottage."

"Yes, and if you hadn't had the premonition, you would have never gotten involved with me," she said.

"It sounds like a circular reference, a closed loop, if it weren't for one thing," Jay said, smiling.

"Which is?"

"The fact that some things are meant to be, just like we were meant to be together, whether as a result of my premonition of Smith, or another cause. Some things are inevitable. And so was me falling in love with you."

Olivia traced his lips with her finger. "I love you, Jay, I think I fell in love with you the first time I saw you in class."

"See? Some things are inevitable." Then he chuckled. "Just like the fact that we're not getting any sleep tonight."

Olivia giggled, and Jay rolled them to bring her underneath him, before he silenced her laughter with his lips on hers.

About the Author

Tina Folsom was born in Germany and has been living in English speaking countries since 1991. Tina has always been a bit of a globe trotter. She lived in Munich, Lausanne, London, New York City, Los Angeles, San Francisco, and Sacramento. She has now made a beach town in Southern California her permanent home with her American husband and her dog.

She's written 50 romance novels in English most of which are translated into German, French, and Spanish.

https://tinawritesromance.com
tina@tinawritesromance.com

facebook.com/TinaFolsomFans
instagram.com/authortinafolsom